The Spaniard's Cross

Sharon K. Garner

Hard Shell Word Factory

To Lee and Beth.
Live well, love much, laugh often.

ISBN: 0-7599-4135-1
Trade Paperback
Published January 2004

© 2003 Sharon K. Garner
eBook ISBN: 0-7599-4134-3
Published October 2003

Hard Shell Word Factory
PO Box 161
Amherst Jct. WI 54407
books@hardshell.com
www.hardshell.com
Cover art © 2003 Dirk A. Wolf
All rights reserved

All characters in this book have no existence outside the imagination of the author, and have no relation whatever to anyone bearing the same name or names. These characters are not even distantly inspired by any individual known or unknown to the author, and all incidents are pure invention.

Prologue

CORNWALL SHOOK OFF the soft spring day like a cat vibrating a wet paw. Low clouds pushed in from the sea, bullying from the horizon the last rays of April sun. Under the threat of rain, the wind moaned to itself.

Limping, Ellie retraced her steps along the pea-gravel pathway that skirted Penwith. It had brought her in orderly fashion from the stone house's carved oak front door to its lead-paned kitchen door. Because she wasn't expected, her knocks went unanswered at both.

She glanced down to see if the plump black cat who'd picked her up at a pub still dogged her every step. Whether or not Traveller the cat appreciated that mental observation and comparison, she reinforced it by following close on Ellie's heels. Uneasiness, which Ellie blamed on second thoughts as much as she blamed the impending storm, settled over her like a heavy cloak. Unable to stop herself, she looked over her shoulder.

Penwith sat at the narrow head of a V-shaped valley. The rent in the fabric of the southern Cornish peninsula rendered the land at Penwith's back into a seamless yet improbable blending of headland meadow and moor. A spindly hedge did little to separate tame, civilized Penwith from the green, tan, yellow, and gray-green expanse. It rippled away into shadows and mist, just as Trev had described it in his letters. She caught a gray-blue glimmer, the small lake where the swans lived.

But something else lingered out there, making itself known to her first on the wind then in her bones. A chill climbed hand over hand up her spine and across her shoulders as whispers of ancient, primeval deeds known only to the moorland reached a place of secret understanding within her. They spoke of old gods and dark misdeeds.

She shivered. "I'd better jot this stuff down," she muttered to Traveller, with more bravado than she felt. "Save it for the Penwith brochures. It sets just the right tone, don't you think?"

Turning away, she hurried around the protective corner of the house, black cat in tow.

Chapter One

"BLOODY HELL!"

Deep, resonant, and laden with a potent mixture of surprise, anger, and fear, the voice came from above her—and got through her pain pill-induced doze.

Ellie's eyes popped open to confusion and a heart-pounding panic. Denied a waking moment, she had trouble focusing on the even-featured face hanging over her, blue eyes agog. A thick mass of too-long blond hair topped the sleek, light brown brows and vaguely familiar features.

His gaze fastened on hers. "Oh, thank heaven," he declared, closing those beautiful eyes and bowing his head for an instant.

She used the opportunity to grasp the black thorn walking stick she'd found with her left shoulder in her napping place, the sofa in Penwith's sitting room. She brought its silver handle down with a healthy whack on that cushion of light hair.

Too late she noticed that her attacker was leaning well over and that he was tall. Stunned by the blow, he folded over the high back of the sofa and slithered down onto her, full length, forcing the air from her lungs in a whoosh.

Traveller, who had dibs on the other end of the long sofa, growled and went elsewhere.

Ellie, unfortunately, could not. She froze, fighting for her next breath. When he raised his head to groggily peer at her, she heard herself whimper. The sound roused him into awareness.

He came up onto his elbows, gingerly probing his hair with the long, slim fingers of one hand. "Bloody hell!" he repeated with feeling.

His voice jolted her out of her terror-induced paralysis. If she were being attacked, then she would go down fighting. The rest of the way down, she amended. She hefted the walking stick again, aiming to show this Englishman what American women were made of.

His hand shot out and grabbed her wrist. "What do you think you're doing, Ellie?" he inquired, tossing her weapon of opportunity just out of her reach. "Is this an American greeting custom you never shared in your letters?"

His voice saying her name told her she had probably

misunderstood what was happening here. "Er, defending myself? Trev?" she asked, still woozy from the pills but heartily relieved. "Oh, I'm so glad it's you."

"Really? At this point I'd much rather someone else had been on the receiving end of that walking stick." His voice changed as anger crept in. "So help me, Ellie, if you'd come to Penwith to kill yourself, I'd—I'd—"

"Kill myself?" She worked hard to focus on his face at such close quarters. "Why would I come all the way to England, the trip of a lifetime, to kill myself? What makes you think that?"

She followed his glanced to the low table beside them where she'd set down her pill bottle and empty glass beside the whiskey bottle and the soda bottle already in residence.

"The whiskey. The pills." He paused. "The accident."

Her eyes widened in understanding. "Oh. No, I only took two. With some soda. For my leg. And I'm coming to terms with the a-accident. Really."

She was babbling, so she closed her mouth and took a deep, steadying breath. In this expansion process she noted that the body of her pen pal of 18 years nested quite well with hers, curve to hollow, hollow to curve. Disconcertingly well. Meanwhile, she was aware that his gaze followed the contours of her face, coming to rest on her mouth.

"I'm glad you're finally here, Ellie, but why didn't you tell me you were coming?"

"I wasn't sure when I'd arrive." She was conscious that he watched her lips as she spoke. "Now that I'm at Penwith, may I stay awhile? I can do PR for the tours and the bed and breakfast."

His gaze shot up to meet hers. "Of course you can stay. As long as you like. It's a standing invitation, plus you're an investor. My only investor, by the way. I'd appreciate the PR help, though," he added with a little smile.

"Thanks. Now, could we..."

He tested a strand of her hair between his fingers, judging its silkiness. She watched out of the corner of her eye.

His next words accompanied a look of distracted concern. "Well timed, Ellie. I might need your help with something else. A difficult guest. What do you know about Spaniards?"

She wondered briefly what this foreign guest had done. "Er, they're from Spain? Don't you think—"

The head of a large gnome hove into view above the back of the sofa. She screamed in Trev's face, unable to look away from the creature. When its mouth split in a grin, it changed before her eyes into the wizened features of a small man.

"Evening, guv. Sorry I'm so late. Who's your friend?" He stared down at Ellie with delight evident on his face.

"Reilly, this is my pen friend, Ellie Jaymes, from the States. Ellie, this is Reilly, Penwith's cook."

Trev's tone made her sound like a blue-ribbon show-and-tell exhibit, and that's exactly what she was beginning to feel like. She wondered, as she awkwardly grasped and shook the hand Reilly reached down to her, who else might belly up to the back of the sofa to casually observe them in this compromising position. The difficult guest seemed to be the only one missing.

Reilly's face was wreathed in smiles. "Oh, right." To her he said, still pumping her hand, "Pleased to meet you." To Trev, he commented, "Friendly, these Americans, aren't they?"

Ellie, her face flooding with heat, raised her voice above their casual conversation. "Do you think we could possibly continue this discussion in an upright position, Trev?"

He looked down at her in surprise. "Oh. Sorry, Ellie. Although this was your fault, if you'll recall." His devilish and formidable grin revealed even white teeth and brought glints to the dark blue streaks in his azure eyes.

He removed himself from both her body and the sofa in one graceful move, while asking Reilly to find them something to eat. She sat up and shot backwards into the corner where the sofa arm and back met. With a glance at the walking stick on the floor near her end of the sofa, Trev settled himself in the opposite corner, recently vacated by the cat.

"Was that Traveller? From the pub outside Avallen?" He asked his questions as though everything that had happened so far was perfectly normal.

She gamely ignored her Alice-through-the-looking-glass feeling. "Yes, I stopped there to ask directions to Penwith. She climbed into the car and refused to get out again."

"Ah, kittens," he said, as if that explained everything.

"Kittens," she repeated faintly. "The man at the pub said she'd come back there in her own good time."

Trev snorted. "Oh, she will. I'll bet Josh didn't tell you that Traveller only roams when she's about to deliver, did he? Her progeny are spread all over south Cornwall." He paused then flashed her a devastating smile. "But where have my manners gone? Welcome to Penwith, Ellie."

She blinked, hesitating while she gathered in her straying thoughts. His smile had sent them scuttling in a different direction. "Thank you, Trev. It's beautiful, the little I've seen of it. When nobody answered my hellos, I came straight in here and didn't roam around. I hope you don't mind my making myself at home like this. I didn't want to stay in the car in the storm."

He held her gaze with his own. "*Mi casa, su casa*, Ellie. You know that."

She did know. She'd felt the house welcome her when she had mustered up the courage to open the massive oak front door and venture inside.

She studied him, processing the sound of his voice and adapting to a three-dimensional Trev. She'd met her childhood pen pal only on paper, online, and in photographs until this moment.

"I'm sorry about what I thought was happening just now, and for not recognizing you at first. I'll blame it on the pain pills and on waking too quickly. I take them only when I have to. The drive down from London nearly did me in, with help from a lorry or two."

She had meant to make a slow journey to the West Country of England, more of a sedate meander toward Cornwall, one where she would call ahead and prepare herself for this meeting. But when her feet touched British soil, they had attached themselves to the clutch and gas pedal of a small rental car and brought her in an undignified, headlong rush to Penwith and Trev, unannounced.

He smiled again and she felt herself relax. "Your reaction was understandable under the circumstances. I'm sorry I frightened you. If I'd known you were coming, I'd have given you a proper welcome."

"Oh, this one was memorable," she said around a grin.

He sent her a warm look. "It was indeed. I'm really glad you're here, Ellie." Then the warmth left his face. "Unfortunately, that guest I mentioned is arriving soon, plus I invited an old school chum down to help out in the gardens. We won't have the place to ourselves."

She hurried to reassure him. "I didn't come to Penwith to be entertained, Trev. We'll find time to talk, that's all I need. I'll help with the difficult guest. In fact, I'll put my hand to whatever I can, including kitchen duty, if Reilly will have me. Just as long as you're sure my being here isn't a problem." Her heart did a slow and not very graceful dive to her feet at the look on his face.

"It's certainly not a problem," he protested. "It's just...I would have prepared myself emotionally, if I'd known. I've looked forward to a visit from you for so long." He cocked his head and gave her a lopsided grin. "Does that make sense?"

It made a lot of sense. It was difficult for her to adjust in person to this stranger she understood so well on paper. Their years of words did nothing to prepare her for this moment. "It makes sense. I'm feeling the strangeness of it myself."

Trev was a handsome man, no doubt about it. From their brief but intimate contact, she knew that long, lean body, half-reclining with loose-limbed grace on the opposite end of the sofa, was healthy, discreet muscle, nicely covered tonight by well-worn jeans and an Irish wool sweater. And those two-tone blue eyes....

His gaze moved from her denim-clad legs to her face. "So, how are you, Ellie, and what finally brought you to Penwith?"

That brought her back to reality. She looked away a moment before answering. "I don't have a clue how I am. Really. And that's why I'm here. All I know is that I can't settle down to my old life, and it's been more than a year since the a-accident." She paused, amazed that eight letters could hold so much horror and pain, and that she still stumbled over the word.

"I needed to get away from everything for a while, and Penwith was where I wanted to be. So, I took a leave of absence from the library and here I am, ready to work. My leg has healed. I need to walk a lot to strengthen it. It's a little painful tonight from the long drive and your English spring weather."

Spying the whiskey bottle, he asked, "Do you mind?" He poured a small measure into her used glass and tipped it down. "This has been a strange day. Our first guest is arriving tomorrow, I was delayed in Treborne, and Reilly stayed longer than expected at his friend's cottage. I'm sorry you arrived to an empty house."

"You didn't expect me. But with that storm out there, I was grateful the door wasn't locked."

He set down the glass. "It's clear now. You know Cornwall. A shower every day and two on Sunday. I realize you're probably exhausted and just want your bed, but you should eat a bite. I'm sure Reilly has something ready by now. Are you game?"

"Yes, please. My nap revived me and now I'm hungry. May I take a quick shower and change my clothes first?"

"My manners have apparently deserted me. Of course you'll want to get out of your traveling clothes. The food is probably something cold anyway."

She looked away from his warm, unwavering observation and caught a glimpse of her former weapon. "I'm really sorry about the walking stick, Trev. Did I hurt you?"

He stood up then pulled her gently to her feet. "No, it brought back fond memories."

He led the way into the hall where she'd dropped her bags beside the front door. She followed more slowly, appreciating the way he moved, walking to a beat only he could hear.

"My dear old maiden aunt used to wield that very stick in much the same manner upon my young head." He bent over to heft her bags and looked up at her, his eyes asking if she remembered that letter.

She did. "So that's Great-Aunt Fiona's walking stick?" She ended with a husky laugh.

She watched him blink then swallow as the sound echoed into the hall behind him. Then he turned with his load to switch on the strong entrance hall chandelier. In its exquisite gleam, Traveller stared down at them with indignant yellow eyes from the top of the stairs while Ellie looked around with delight. Trev seemed pleased with the approving sounds she made.

Penwith wasn't a huge manor house but it had grace and character. She followed him up the polished, graceful wooden staircase that swept upward then split, leading to halls on the right and left on the next floor. White fan vaulting soared above the main hall. The ceiling between was painted a soft blue to highlight its delicate curves. The wide blue and gold patterned carpet runner on the floor and stairs picked up the color in the ceiling but in a darker tone.

A small gallery, with a carved handrail and banisters in dark wood, swept across the top of the staircase. The halls, leading to the wings of the U-shaped house, were mere shadows on each side of it. Trev turned to the right-hand stairs then led her down the right wing hall to a pretty room.

By that time, she understood and heartily agreed with Trev's decision to use light, bright colors to offset the dark, carved wood paneling throughout the house. This large room's accents, draperies, and bed covering were in a cream cabbage rose-pattern with touches of pink and sage, with a cream and sage Aubusson carpet underfoot. The effect was relaxing, yet formal.

He put her small bags on the floor beside the bed and the large one on a luggage rack against the wall. Traveller hopped onto the bed covering, turned around once, then settled down in a furry apostrophe. She was so black that she became a featureless shadow when she closed her eyes.

Trev indicated the cat. "Do you mind?"

"Not if you don't. I've enjoyed her company." She looked around again. "This is a lovely room, Trev."

"I imagined you staying in this room the whole time I worked on it. It's the first one I renovated."

Her mouth opened in surprise at his words and at the gentle color flowing beneath his skin. She spoke into the awkward silence. "You say you have a guest arriving. A paying guest?"

A frown creased his brow. "Oh, he's paying all right. We're not officially open as a bed and breakfast, yet this Spaniard insists on staying here and using us as a hotel. He'll be attending an estate sale near Treborne in a few days."

She sat down on the tufted bench at the foot of the bed. "He insists? Is that why you say he's difficult?"

"He's been very pushy and stubborn about staying at Penwith." He jammed his hands into his jeans pockets. "I quoted an exorbitant rate to put him off. He didn't even pause before he paid it. In advance. I'm trying to be gracious. At the price he's paying, we're including lunch and dinner for his convenience."

"But how did he hear about Penwith?" She frowned in puzzlement. "Have you done any advertising?"

"Not yet. Maybe he heard about us by word of mouth. We've already received a few reservations that way for our official opening at the end of next month. That's why I'm putting on the push now. I have six weeks to get the final touches in place. We're almost there."

"I can see that. Since I'll be doing your PR, I'll find out from him how he heard about us, er, Penwith."

"I've just realized that I've never spoken with him. I dealt with his personal assistant throughout." He shrugged. "Maybe he'll turn out to be all right once I meet him. He's probably a frail, elderly little man. Maybe an executive fighting retirement and accustomed to getting his way." The heavy frown was back. "I hope that's all he is."

He moved away as he continued to speak. "There's a door in the paneling where this hall intersects with the gallery. Behind it are stairs that will bring you directly to the kitchen. I'll see you shortly." With a brief smile, he was gone.

Ellie stared after him before she moved to the tall, thick wooden door he'd just closed. Trev had added a modern lock, which probably meant a spare key or master key downstairs somewhere. Mindlessly, she toyed with the ancient slide bolt. It moved soundlessly and smoothly, despite its age.

She sighed and turned toward her bags. Instead of opening them, however, she sat down on the bed and reached out to touch the cat. She hadn't taken any liberties thus far, but Traveller's shining black fur made an inviting, pretty contrast against the light tones of the bed covering.

Her furry traveling companion was at Penwith now because earlier that day Ellie had forgotten in a pub car park that she was in the British Isles. She had opened the left-side door to climb in. The black cat had brushed past her, sat down on the passenger seat, and refused to get out again.

When Ellie recovered, she had gone back inside to ask about the cat. The owner told her that Traveller belonged to no one and, when the mood was on her, climbed into a vehicle of her choosing for a look at some new country. Eventually she would return to the vicinity of the pub, in her own good time. He offered to remove her, but by that time Ellie was delighted with the story and pleased that she had been chosen. She had welcomed her feline passenger on the last leg of her journey.

She snapped out of her reverie when she caught a glimpse of herself in the dressing table mirror across the room. "Oh, no! This is how Trev first saw me?" She moaned softly at the realization. No wonder he had studied her so intently when she wanted a shower and a change of clothes.

Her brandy-colored eyes returned her horrified stare through a curtain of red spider webs. Some eye drops were definitely in order. Her pale oval face was framed by thick, straight brown hair badly in need of attention and a brush. Her rumpled clothing bore stains from meals she'd shared with rough, friendly lorry drivers during her rest stops. She'd developed a soft spot for truck drivers after the accident.

"I wanted the moment, and me, to be perfect for our first meeting, and look at me." She paused, stroking the cat. "What am I going to do, Traveller, now that I know for sure? Any suggestions?"

Ellie reconsidered the two reasons she had come to Penwith and found both were still sound. First, whatever Trev had to offer her was essential for her to heal and move on. She was certain of that. No compromises, no explanations, no embarrassment. When she thought she was dying, she had wanted Trev, she had called out for Trev.

Second, coming here was an act of faith. All her life she'd been a firm believer that the farthest distance between any two points was between the head and the heart. That's what made this confirmed truth so hard to accept, shaking her to her very core. She reeled under the knowledge that she, Ellie Jaymes, mild-mannered librarian closing in on 30, was in love with a man she knew only through his written words.

The cat addressed Ellie's question by rolling over and presenting her round belly for rubbing. "Ah, kittens," Ellie repeated Trev's words, then she obliged.

During the soothing interlude, Ellie mentally answered her own question. She would find out if Trev had romantic feelings for her, without letting him know her feelings for him, in case they were one-sided. Her tired brain reeled under the convoluted thought.

One thing was clear. She wouldn't risk losing Trev's friendship. He meant too much to her. If he didn't love her, or didn't fall in love with her, then she'd return to her apartment and to the library where she worked. It would be time to get serious about a man on her side of the Atlantic Ocean.

She dragged herself upright through sheer will power. If she showered now, she would probably drown. The nap had definitely been a temporary fix. She stole another look at herself in the mirror and decided to risk it.

The stinging cascade of hot water revived her. Standing in it, she reviewed the dizzying moment more than a year ago when she suspected she was in love with her pen pal of 18 years, a man she'd never met.

It had been one of those special days when she looked her best, felt her best, and the world had dealt her its best. From the blue airmail envelope from England in her mailbox to a parking space right in front of the library, everything had gone her way.

She was in a playful mood when Alan, a publisher's sales rep, picked her up for dinner. She reviewed her satisfying day for him and added, "'Bad rice, bad rice,'" the deceive-the-jealous-gods line from Han Suyin's *A Many-Splendored Thing*, invoked so the gods wouldn't snatch away her happiness.

She and Trev had shared the quote with each other years before. They needed only those four words to convey a wealth of meaning about thankfulness, good luck, and being blessed in some way. Alan had simply stared at her in the candlelight, suspecting the wine had gone to her head. And she had encouraged his misgivings by owlishly looking back at him. In that instant of time, she guessed. Trev?

Then, before she had gathered enough courage to accept Trev's invitation to come to England, a chain reaction pile-up on a foggy highway laid her up, mentally and physically, for seven months. Trev's almost-daily letters and her nightly dreams of him and Penwith were the only things that made the pain and the memories bearable.

Now, tonight, she had met the man of her dreams in the flesh. Tonight, the Penwith that had welcomed her in her dreams welcomed her within its ancient walls. Trev and Penwith were everything she wanted and needed them to be. And so much more.

And, as dreams went, they both looked like keepers.

Chapter Two

CLEAN AND REFRESHED, she stepped out of her room into the hall. Ancient iron torch holders set at regular intervals high on the walls had been adapted for electric lights and glowed softly to guide her. The house below the gallery was dark when she peered over the handrail. She searched out the almost invisible door set into the paneling where the right-wing hall turned off the gallery. The wooden stairs behind it were solid, except for one that creaked, and her feet whispered down them to the kitchen below.

She stopped short just inside the swinging door at the bottom and gave a low whistle. A study in contrasts, the large room, by her estimate, took up the back two-thirds of the first floor, right wing of the house. Occupying most of one wall was a stone fireplace with a crane, an array of hooked arms that swung over the fire for cooking. There were even side ovens. Iron kettles and pot ovens that would have hung over the flames in the old days now sat cold but decorative on the hearth.

On the opposite wall the current century was solidly in place. All the mod cons, a gas cooker, double wall ovens, a full-size refrigerator/freezer, a microwave, and a double sink with cupboards above, filled the area. Two dressers sat against each remaining wall. Sturdy crockery and fine china pieces sat on the dresser shelves above the drawers. Colorful plaited rag rugs filled strategic spots around the flagstone floor.

Candles burned at one end of the scrubbed oak farm table in the center of the floor. When he saw her, Trev took two brown bottles from the refrigerator, putting one at each place setting.

He smiled and gestured toward the candles. "Reilly has declared this a celebration. And so it is." He took her hand and raised her fingers to his lips.

She saw in slow motion that her hand and his lips grew closer, touching for one potent moment and sending something that felt like living fire up her arm. That touch and the accompanying look in Trev's eyes made it a warm, true homecoming for her.

He pulled out her chair and she sat down before a platter of sliced roasted chicken, round slices of rich yellow cheese, and crusty bread made, she didn't doubt, by Reilly's own hands. The brown bottle held cider. Trev pointed out the usual condiments, plus a crock of freshly churned butter from a neighboring farm.

"Reilly's new, isn't he?" She didn't remember Trev mentioning Reilly in his letters to her.

He went still. "Yes. He's a transplanted Londoner whose mother was Cornish. I got to know him when he was a cook on one of the North Sea oil platforms. He was fine when on duty, but when he had leave, he drank himself into a stupor. Then he retired and was onshore all the time, which was a problem, so he signed himself into rehab. We kept in touch. I offered him this position when he got out. So far, so good."

Her eyes stung as she listened to the story. "You have a kind heart, Trev. Traveller and I are glad you take in strays."

He shrugged. "Solid friendships and second chances are two things I heartily believe in."

She fought the urge to grab his face with both hands and plant a smacking kiss on his forehead. Maybe a little lower.

"Our first meal together," she ventured then took a slice of bread, a round of cheese, and a piece of chicken from the platter.

He denied it with a shake of his head. "I always read your letters as soon as I get them, then I reread them when I eat alone. I've had many, many meals with you, Ellie."

She was pleased that her written words had given as much pleasure and companionship to him as his had given to her. "I do the same thing. This is our first face-to-face meal then."

He raised his bottle of cider. "Cheers, Ellie. And God bless our respective postal systems," he added with a grin.

"Cheers," she whispered and touched her cider bottle to his.

The cider was dry, not bitter, and quenched her thirst for the first time since her arrival in England. The cheese, distinctive because of the particular water and fertile soil in the area where it had been made, was real English cheddar, not the American version Ellie had been accustomed to all her life. Reilly's bread was crusty and fine-textured. She was hungrier than she thought. They didn't speak again for several minutes while Ellie made these delectable discoveries.

Trev broke the easy silence between them. "How old were we when we started writing to each other?"

"I was your nine-year-old pen friend, and you were my ten-year-old pen pal. I was afraid you wouldn't want to write to me because I was a girl and younger than you." She smiled at the memory of her pen-wielding young self at nine.

His gaze moved over her face and hair, and she felt every moment of his warm journey of discovery. "We clicked right away. Remember? Your photographs don't do you justice, by the way. I don't know why you dislike your hair so much. It's lovely." He raised a hand to touch it then appeared to reconsider.

"Really?" Tears were suddenly very close. He liked her thick, straight hair! "There's so much of it and it just...hangs there."

He shook his head in disbelief. "But it doesn't. It shines in the light and moves like a living thing when you move."

Feeling her face grow warm, she concentrated on her plate of food. "Hmmm, I'll have to reconsider my hair, I guess. And I think the same about your photographs, that they don't do you justice."

"Speaking of photographs, I carried the first photograph you sent me in my pocket. My mother put it through the washing machine. Do you remember? You sent me another." His eyes lit up with a warm glow when he laughed. She had known they would.

"I remember." She hesitated then reached into the pocket of the soft knit slacks she'd slipped on with her sweater. Her fingers found the edge of the photograph she'd put there before she left her room. "This is the first one you sent to me. Do you remember it? Nobody washed it."

He stared at the thin boy in the photograph. "So many wasted... So many years ago," he corrected in a whisper. Then his voice changed, becoming brisk and friendly. "You should have come over on holiday years ago, you know."

It hurt that he put on a jolly tone and hurried past things important to her. "I know, but the Atlantic is an equal opportunity ocean, you know. Did life get in your way, too?"

"Life most definitely got in my way. You're here now, and I can show you Penwith and the gardens and Avallen, all of Cornwall and England, if we can find the time."

She put down her sandwich. "Please don't compromise the work on Penwith because of me. We'll manage local sightseeing when we can. And did you say gardens? Are you restoring them, too? I thought you gave up gardening when you had to spend so much time away."

"Give up gardening? Never. And do you still enjoy sitting up half the night reading?" His eyes glinted softly in the candlelight.

"Give up reading? Never. It's an occupational hazard for librarians." These words they exchanged in person made her breathless. "I want to read every new book that crosses my desk."

He nodded and she realized he understood as no one else ever could. "I want the gardens to be part of the tour, but they're a real challenge, Ellie. Reilly is a dab hand at it, so he helped with the planning and some of the work. And Annie, too. She's Reilly's friend who comes in every day to do for us, keep the place clean. I'm depending on my school friend Geoff to rent the correct machines and do the heavy work in the gardens, if he ever turns up. With Geoff in the gardens and you doing the PR for us...Thank heavens I'm blessed with good friends."

She smiled and it turned into the yawn she'd been fighting for some time.

"Time for you to get some rest. Tomorrow the Spaniard will be here." He went still again for a moment. "How very strange to say that, to think that."

"Why? Because he's your first guest?"

"Not that. There was another Spaniard connected with Penwith once upon a time. I'll tell you about him when the time is right." He gave her his hand to help her out of her chair then he looked at the flagstone floor all around them.

"What's the matter? Did you lose something?" she asked, puzzled.

"The blackthorn walking stick isn't handy, is it? I'd like very much to give you a hug of welcome and goodnight. If I scare you or embarrass you, you might hit me again."

His enormous vitality, which pictures and paper and computer monitor failed to capture, flowed into her.

She smiled at his teasing but her cheeks tingled at his words. "Go ahead. Scare me, embarrass me, whatever. I'm prepared." She held up her arms and walked into his outstretched ones. "It's so nice to meet you at last, Trev."

She felt...comfortable in his arms, and a tiny voice inside prodded her. *A kiss on the cheek could turn into something else entirely, if one of you turned just a little.* Then, as he stepped back and dropped a kiss on her cheek, the chaste peck *did* turn into something else. And she wouldn't place bets on which one of them made it happen.

A flurry of sensations swept over her, all of them strangely familiar. She recognized those soft, warm lips. She remembered that hard, muscled body. She responded anew to promises his mouth made against hers. In that uncanny moment in his arms, she discovered that Trevor Sinclair wasn't a stranger to her or to her body.

Some veiled part of her recognized his kiss and the feel of him pressed against her. Yet no man had felt like this to her, or made her feel this way, before. She pulled back in astonishment, wondering if he felt any of those things. She blinked up at him, allowing her puzzlement and wonder to show on her face.

He appeared dazed, but then he frowned and whispered an apology. "I'm so sorry, Ellie. I guess we're both exhausted. Sleep well."

Nodding wordlessly, she turned toward the back stairs, taking her disappointed and bemused self to bed. Trev obviously hadn't felt a thing.

AT EIGHT THE next morning, Traveller woke her, pacing and crying at the bedroom door. Ellie put on a silk kimono wrap and fuzzy slippers, planning to slip down the back stairs to let out the cat. Instead, from the gallery, she saw that the huge front door stood open to the warm, fresh morning breeze. Traveller's dark form glided down the stairs and out into the morning without a backward glance. A pang of sadness surprised Ellie when she wondered if she'd ever see the black cat again.

She dressed in jeans and a long-sleeved tee shirt, then grabbed her clipboard and went down the back stairs to find breakfast.

A tiny figure reared up out of one of the substantial rocking chairs on each side of the fireplace hearth. Ellie squeaked in alarm and dropped the clipboard.

The elfin woman, with dyed black hair, a tight perm, and a full set of store-bought teeth, greeted her. "Good morning, miss. Reilly went to the shops. I'm to fix your breakfast, should you come down before he gets back. And here you are."

Ellie doubted the woman could have remained upright in yesterday's blustery storm. She picked up her clipboard and moved farther into the room, being careful not to step on her or knock her over.

"You must be Annie. I'm Ellie Jaymes. Call me Ellie. I'm Trev's friend, and I'm working here, too."

"Right you are, Miss Ellie. What would you like for your breakfast, then?" She tilted her head to one side in a birdlike gesture.

Before Ellie answered, the back door opened. Reilly bustled in with net carrier bags almost as big as he was. He repeated Annie's greeting, told Ellie he'd be with her in a tick, and set about unloading his booty.

In the light of day and standing upright, Ellie saw that Reilly was much shorter than her own five feet eight inches, yet he stood a full head above Annie. His black hair, dyed to match Annie's, was pulled back into a thin ponytail on the back of his neck. Against the contrast of his dark hair, his light blue eyes, constantly moving, shot lasers of light in time with his words.

"Annie, this is the guv's pen friend from the States. While she's here, she'll let the day trippers and tourists know about Penwith." He harrumphed before he continued. Ellie had never heard anyone harrumph before. "You're welcome in my kitchen anytime, Miss Jaymes. Just remember it's *my* kitchen and we'll get on just fine."

She nodded. "No arguments here, Reilly. I'm kitchen impaired most of the time, anyway. And please, both of you, call me Ellie. Is Trev around?"

"He's getting the lads started in the left wing. The work can't stop just because we're invaded by a...Spaniard." The way he said it, the word had four letters.

Heavy footsteps thundered down the stairs and punctuated Reilly's last words. The little man moved to the stove as Trev, like a fresh sea wind, burst into the room.

Reilly continued his conversation with no one in particular. "Can't stand bloody Spaniards, not since—"

"Reilly!" Trev said it softly but so intensely that it jarred like a shout in the quiet kitchen. Ellie stared at him in shock. When he noticed her look, he said, "Ellie, you're up early. No sign of the Armada yet?"

She spoke into the awkward moment. "Not that I've seen, but then I just got here myself."

"Right." He rubbed his hands together gleefully. "Let's take advantage of the lull. After one of Reilly's amazing omelets, how about a tour of Avallen before the invasion?"

Before she answered, Reilly, in another conversation with himself, paused in his attempt to beat helpless eggs into submission. "I wanted to make damask cream for dinner tonight, but the cream had gone off. The piskies got it."

Ah, safe ground at last. She knew about piskies from Trev. The Cornish household fairies took the blame for any foodstuffs that spoiled in the kitchen.

"Cream," Trev repeated without inflection. "Are you saying you need cream from the village?"

"No, I don't need cream from the village. I've just been in, haven't I. I'll not start the roast, though, until I see the whites of this

Spaniard's eyes," he declared.

Dazed, Ellie watched Annie, who beamed at Reilly through the whole exchange, pick up her cleaning supplies and start up the back stairs. With a sparkle in his eyes that told her to go with the flow, Trev invited her to sit down at the table. At first bite, she complimented Reilly on the delicious, feather-light omelet he served.

When they had finished, Trev opened the back door to the morning. To Reilly, he said, "If the Spaniard shows up before I get back, register him, show him to his room, and feed him. We'll find lunch in Avallen."

They climbed the path that led out of the valley and onto the meadow-moor behind the house. The hand Trev offered her over the steep spots was warm and calloused from the work he'd been doing on the house. She knew he'd been a man of action in his fieldwork too. As a geologist for an oil company, he had chafed at desk time, straining to be out of doors or with the men on the oil platforms.

"If you want to walk regularly to strengthen your leg, then it's two miles one way to Avallen by the moor path or a three-mile walk by the cliff road."

She remembered the cliff road below them as the last lap of her journey. But the last leg of her three-hundred-mile trip from London had truly begun when she crossed the Tamar River. After that, the sharp horizon had curved, and she felt like she was driving downhill. She had recognized the names of towns and villages on the signs because she'd read them in books or Trev had mentioned them: Bodmin, Truro, Redruth.

Soon, rolling hills had given way to moorland. She found Cornwall's middle bleak and bumpy, dotted with pyramids of china-clay waste, reminders of one of Cornwall's shining hours. However, other remnants of past glories, the gaunt chimney-like structures of abandoned tin mines, reminded her of the ruins of churches and castles.

She eventually took a road that headed south, to Avallen and the sea, and found the south coast of Cornwall softer, wetter, and greener. The streets, lanes, and footpaths in and near villages were narrow and irregular. Winding field walls and hedges enclosed tiny, oddly shaped fields. The cliffs near the sea were steep meadows rather than the rocky faces of the north coast.

Trev interrupted her reverie when he paused at a place where they could look down on Penwith and the two terraced gardens that stepped down away from it toward the sea. They shared the silence, punctuated by wind, sea, and gulls.

Trev's ancestors had built the house in a valley, and the cliff road below turned to follow it inland, descending toward Penwith. The granite house with its tall, square chimneys and slate roof sat at the valley's head, between its protective sides.

The edges of the valley were wooded and green. Trev described the lushness as a mixture of Cornish elms, sycamores, and, because of the Gulf Stream bathing the shores of Cornwall, a few palm trees. The trees rose to the rippling edges of the moor. Standing sentinel at the edge of the sea in the distance were the gaunt stone and brick ruins of the engine house of the Prudy's Hope tin mine. She admired its graceful, tapering smokestack with the English Channel as its backdrop.

"Your home is beautiful, Trev. Magical," she said with reverence in her voice. She glanced at him and watched the wind ruffle his thick hair, wondering if she would ever know what it felt like to do the same thing with her fingers.

"Beauty and magic are expensive," he replied. "Most of the money my father left me went for inheritance taxes. I've lived simply, saved as much as I could, and I'm happy to say, invested wisely, all the while staying on top of the upkeep of the place. This scheme of mine has to pay, Ellie, or it's back to the oil platforms I go. I could lose Penwith. The insurance premiums to cover the tours and bed and breakfast are outrageous."

She looked down on the stone house, a jewel in the setting of the valley, and knew it would destroy him to have to sell it to a private buyer or give it up to the National Trust.

"I know how much Penwith means to you, Trev. I'll do everything I can to help you make this dream come true." She paused then repeated the house's name quietly. "Remind me. You must have told me what it means at some point."

He looked down at her and grinned. "Penwith was an eleventh-century section of Cornwall. It means 'headland of slaughter.'" He laughed out loud when her eyes widened.

"How could I forget that? It's definitely going in the brochures. What a historical name for a house!"

Below them on the cliff road, two vehicles appeared. Trev tensed as a long, low sports car ate up the sharp curves, followed by the local taxi, an ancient vehicle, lumbering along some distance behind. Both pulled onto the forecourt at Penwith's front, stopping beside Penwith's Land Rover and Ellie's rental car.

Trev heaved a mighty sigh as he watched the activity. "I really ought to go back."

She would be positive, for Trev's sake, while feeling stinging disappointment. "Then let's go back and welcome Penwith's first paying guest. This is a grand moment. We should take pictures. I can see Avallen another time."

They turned back in the direction they'd just come.

"And we really ought to return your rental to Penzance soon." Trev's words were a world away from the look on his face. "You can use the Rover and save some money."

With a sinking feeling, she acknowledged what those two vehicles down there meant. Their short time alone at Penwith was at an end.

Chapter Three

THEY ARRIVED, BREATHLESS, at the back door then continued at a trot around the path to the front. Traveller sat washing herself in the sun on the doorstep. Ellie hung back to stroke her and to catch her breath.

The front door remained open, and Penwith's first paying guest stood in the hall in a shaft of sunlight. Ellie leaned against the doorjamb and observed him amidst the flurry of activity inside. She remembered Trev's fanciful description of the man.

Frail? He was a picture of robust health.

Elderly? Mid-thirties, she'd guess.

Little? This was a *big* Spaniard who could easily pass for one of Cornwall's exotic, black-haired residents, except for the silk tailored suit and the gold flashing on his fingers, wrists, and at his throat. The suit's material fitted snugly across his broad shoulders and thighs.

Man? Most definitely. She could smell the testosterone from where she stood.

An executive? No doubt in her mind.

Retired, or close to it? No way. Nor was he retiring in his manner.

Used to getting what he wants? If it wasn't given, he'd take it.

She straightened when she realized he was looking at her with a mixture of male appreciation and watchful expectation in his dark eyes.

Trev noticed, too. His smile was forced. "This is Ellie Jaymes, a friend visiting from the States. Ellie this is Sebastian Reynaldos from Madrid."

The Spaniard stepped forward long before Trev stopped talking. "El-lie," he repeated, pronouncing it in two distinct syllables and with an accent. It sounded good. He lifted her hand and placed a warm kiss on the back of it.

Ellie gasped as a jolt barreled up her arm, not as good as a Trev-induced jolt but certainly not puny. Was there static electricity on a warm, moist English spring morning? She feared his lips might continue their journey, so she pulled away her hand. His deep brown eyes confidently held her gaze.

"Yes. Well," Trev murmured. "Let me show you to your room."

Reilly, pale and trembling, had scurried outside as soon as Trev appeared, nearly bowling Ellie over in his haste. He now stood ramrod straight, talking to the taxi driver and helping the man unload the bags. Trev joined them to carry the luggage upstairs. Sebastian Reynaldos, who merely watched them all, had a lot of baggage. She took the smallest bag and followed at a distance. At least Penwith's first paying guest carried his own laptop computer case, she noticed.

Without consciously doing so, her gaze found Trev's butt, assessing it in his snug jeans. Very nice. In the spirit of competition, the Spaniard's wasn't bad either, the bit that showed beneath his suit jacket as he climbed ahead of her. This needed further comparison, she decided.

Sebastian Reynaldos' well-modulated voice echoed in the vaulted ceiling above the stairs. "I have business interests I must look after while I'm here. Do you have computer ports in the rooms?"

Trev was slightly winded by his burden. "No, but there's one in the library for guests' use. It's private there. Feel free to use all the downstairs rooms. The kitchen is Reilly's domain, though."

Hah! This man wouldn't know what a kitchen was for.

She wondered if she said it aloud because the Spaniard suddenly stopped on the stairs and looked back, catching her deep in her second round of comparison. He shot her a knowing smile.

"How was the journey down?" she blurted. "I did the drive yesterday."

"The fine weather today is bringing out the...day-trippers, I believe you call them." He almost sneered.

Ellie gave him a bright smile as she passed him. "I'm glad to hear it. Tourists and day-trippers are important to us."

Trev gave the Spaniard the room next to hers. She put down his bag beside the door and turned to leave. Sebastian Reynaldos lounged in the doorway, blocking her exit. His eyes swept her from head to toe. His look told her he liked what he saw.

She glanced beyond him to where Trev questioned Reilly. "What time is lunch for our guest, Reilly?" Trev wiggled his eyebrows at the older man, who suddenly appeared mute as he watched Sebastian.

"A cold collation will be served from noon to one o'clock in the dining room," Reilly stated, loudly and formally then scuttled away.

Sebastian stepped into the hall and bowed her out of his room. Ellie made a mental note to avoid the dining room during that hour. She followed Reilly's example and took the main stairs down, although not at Reilly's breakneck speed. For some reason, she didn't want Sebastian Reynaldos to know about the hidden door in the paneling.

She breathed a sigh of relief when she reached the kitchen's cozy security. "Is there anything I can help you with, Reilly? Are you all right?" She made a move toward him.

Perspiration stood out on his forehead. "Fine, miss. Just a little under the weather this morning. And no, thank you, I can manage. I'll give him the cold sliced chicken and cheese left from last night and a nice vegetable tray." At that moment, Trev joined them. "Will you and Miss Ellie be in for lunch after all, guv?"

"No, we will not. Are you game, Ellie? Avallen awaits and it's just a little after eleven." He held out his hand to her and she gave him hers.

SOON THEY WERE walking along Avallen's narrow main road, the High Street. It snaked between venerable cottages, square and solid, giving the impression they could stand another four or five hundred years. Some of them, but only those in protected nichés, had thatch coming down to the tops of their leaded windows. They reminded her of neatly trimmed heads of hair. Most of them, however, had slate roofs to withstand the wind and weather.

The business area was a row of glass-fronted shops that included a lace shop, a bakery with golden loaves of fresh bread in the windows, a butcher's shop, a greengrocers, and a combination chemist/candy shop that advertised full-cream fudge alongside the fiber drinks and antacids.

A double cottage in the square behind the High Street housed a doctor's office and the police station. A big granite building that bore a striking resemblance to a mother hen sitting amongst her chicks was a combination library, town hall, and post office. The square stone tower of St. Matthew's Church watched over everything from a distance.

She saw the village's name on one of the shop signs. "Avallen is Cornish for 'apple tree.' Right?"

"You get an A, Ellie. There are still traces of the apple orchards that once surrounded the village. Some think Avallen might be the true Avalon of the King Arthur legends."

The town was busy with morning shoppers, and the sidewalks were crowded. Every few feet Trev stopped to pass the time of day with someone and to introduce Ellie. She matched faces to the names he had mentioned to her through the years.

One face in particular, a lovely young woman with dark hair and eyes, made her think of the Spaniard and warm, sunny climates. "Is she a native of Cornwall, Trev?"

"Born and bred. The Cornish believe local men and women with dark, exotic looks are descendants of Spanish sailors who washed up on the beaches after the Spanish Armada was defeated in fifteen eighty-eight."

By the time she visited every shop, if not to buy then to browse, she was starved. Their hunger drove them to The Fair Trader pub. As they approached it, Trev showed her the broad, steep smugglers steps that led to black rocks washed by the sea below. They passed up the outdoor seating on the flagstone terrace and opted for the privacy offered inside.

"This is an old pilchard cellar," Trev told her as they walked through the public bar. He gestured toward their feet. "The grooves along the floor caught the oil dripping from the salted fish hung above to cure. There's a huer's hut monument, a pilchard fishermen's lookout, at Newquay on the north coast. A man on duty raised the hue and cry when the fish were running. I'll add it to my list of Things to Show Ellie."

He led her upstairs to the private bar where they ordered fresh crab cake sandwiches and half pints of the dark, fruity mild bitter Trev had bragged about. While they waited, Ellie admired The Fair Trader's low-beamed ceiling, slab floor, and the brass implements hanging above the fireplace benches.

Matthew Trelawny, the innkeeper, brought their food on a tray. "I heard you was here for a visit, miss. Welcome to The Fair Trader."

News of her presence had spread quickly. Annie and Riley's doing, she guessed.

"Not only did I brag about your bitter in my letters, Matthew, but I told Ellie that The Fair Trader has a colorful history." Trev winked at her.

"No more so than many other places round here, including Penwith." Matthew Trelawney wiped his work-roughened hands on his spotless white apron. "This here cottage was a smugglers den, miss. The goods was carried up the steps from yon beach on the backs of men or on the backs of greased ponies."

The landlord's broad Cornish accent perfectly matched his wide, sunburned face and stocky build. He looked like a fisherman who was helping out in the kitchen.

"Greased ponies?" Ellie wasn't sure she'd heard correctly.

She reached for a paper napkin to write down this interesting fact when she realized she'd left her clipboard at the house. Then she found she had no pen. She balled the napkin in frustration and mentally stored the fact away for later use.

"That's right, miss. Greased ponies was hard to keep a grip on, like, and they was trained to kick to avoid capture. Anyways, the goods was stored in the cellar beneath where you're sitting at this minute. The public bar it is now. It was Penwith's tin mine going that drove men to it, miss."

Someone called his name from downstairs, and he moved away, still talking. "More than brandy and French lace come into our cove. The fishermen needed untaxed salt for drying their pilchards. We'll talk again," he promised, with a wave of his hand and a smile.

Ellie turned to Trev, barely containing her excitement. "I have to interview Matthew Trelawney. The Fair Trader and its history will fascinate guests staying at Penwith. We'll give a coupon for a free drink here, at a special reduced rate we've negotiated with Matthew, of course.

"What he told us just now is exactly what I'm looking for, Trev. Stories like that one tie in with other locations around Penwith yet link to Penwith itself. If we advertise jointly with other business owners, it will hold the costs down for us. Can you think of some others? Do you think they'll agree to meet with me to discuss it?"

His broad grin warmed her. "I suspected you'd have great ideas, Ellie. I've been too busy to think about that end of things. You're officially in charge of Penwith's public relations."

After they took a few bites, Trev asked with studied casualness, "So, what do you think of Reynaldos?"

She hadn't given the Spaniard much thought since she met him. "Love his accent, hate his tailor?"

His grin was worth waiting for. "That suit was a bit much, wasn't it? I hope he tones it down or he'll give the place a bad name." He hesitated. "It's obvious he likes you."

She took and savored a sip of bitter before answering. "Is it? He'll get over it, I'm sure. I won't be lively enough for him. And I'll bet his tastes run to voluptuous and vapid."

"He doesn't know you like I do. And you hold your own in the voluptuous department."

Her cheeks grew warm with pleasure while his grew rosy with embarrassment. "Thank you, kind sir. I'll remember that when I'm feeling...inadequate."

They returned by way of the cliff road. The rugged shoreline fascinated her, and she peppered him with questions as they walked.

"The men who played the smuggling game along this coast must have been very brave." Admiration was heavy in her voice.

"And very desperate." Trev made a sweeping gesture toward the sea. "Let me set the scene for you. It's a dark, moonless night. A cutter or a lugger, which evaded the Revenue cutters, lies off Penwith's cove. Signals are exchanged with the men on shore, and the goods are transferred to smaller boats. The unavoidable sounds are muted: the crunch of the boat's bottom on the shingle beach, the low murmur of voices, footsteps climbing the cliff path.

"They were good at what they did, Ellie, because their lives depended on it. Those few sounds were the only indications that anything out of the ordinary was happening on a soft Cornish night."

AT THE HOUSE, Trev left her in the kitchen and went to check on the workers in the left wing. Her leg felt much better after her walk into Avallen and back. She decided she'd try to do those miles every day. Perhaps she could take Reilly's list to the shops, if he'd let her, or pick up anything he forgot or decided he needed after his own visit.

She picked up her clipboard from the counter where she'd left it earlier and went to the library. She wanted to look for books from which she could pull interesting bits about Penwith, Avallen, and the area in general. She'd settled at the library table with a promising stack beside her when Sebastian, laptop in hand, came in. He'd toned it down to Chinos and a knit polo shirt, a walking advert for men's casual wear.

"Ah, Ellie," he said. "I hope I may call you Ellie, and you must call me Sebastian. Do you know where this port is located?"

She helped him search. With his computer connected, he sat down with it at the desk across the room.

"Would you like to be alone while you conduct your business?" She placed her clipboard on top of her pile of books.

He held up his hands in protest. "No, please stay. You are a delightful addition to the room."

Several times, as she got up and down to fetch books off the shelves or to return them, she felt his eyes on her. Finally, she gathered a stack and went to her room to work. Other than a short tea break with Reilly and Annie in the kitchen, she worked all afternoon, until it was time to get ready for dinner.

When she had packed for this trip, she imagined herself sharing meals with Trev and his workmen, so she hadn't brought anything special from home for a dinner.

However, in London, as she hurried past an airport shop, a dress called out to her from a display window. It was like nothing she'd ever bought or worn before. It was so dramatically plain that it was chic, so chic it was expensive, so expensive it was outrageous, and so outrageous it was irresistible. On impulse, she bought it, along with almost everything displayed with it.

It was a basic little black dress...with attitude. Its length came to just above her knees and ended in a lettuce leaf edging that flicked with every movement of her legs. Its plunging neckline revealed the soft upper curves of her breasts. Her leg wouldn't accept high, high heels, so she had chosen a plain black, low-heeled evening pump to wear with it. A set of pearl-encrusted combs and some pearl costume jewelry had also found their way onto her credit card.

She used the combs now to hold back her hair from her face, added pearl earrings, and a pearl pin on the dress's shoulder, then stood back to gauge the effect.

"Wow!" she said to the mirror, wide-eyed, wondering about the sophisticated woman looking back at her. Pleased, she draped the dress's matching wrap into the crook of each elbow against the April evening's chill then opened her door.

Trev stood on the doorstep, one hand raised, his flexed index finger at the ready to tap on her door. He froze in the act.

Her evening pumps were suddenly glued to the floor. Trev wore a dark navy suit, white shirt, conservative tie...and he looked so good that she gaped like a schoolgirl. She closed her mouth, swallowed, then tried to speak.

He beat her to it. "I—you—" He cleared his throat and tried again. "As my father often said to my mother, 'You look smashing, my dear.'"

She found the compliment strangely touching. Her head jerked in acknowledgement. "And what did she say? No, let me guess. 'Likewise, my dear?'"

Trev noticed his bent finger in front of his face and dropped his hand to his side. "Got it in one."

She wanted...no, needed...to hear *his* words, even if she had to extract them, one by one. "Now that I know what your father would have said, tell me what *you* would say to me now, Trev."

"I think you look smashing, Ellie," he whispered. "Kittens and Christmas and sinfully rich cake for tea, all wrapped up in one delightful package." There was a glint in his eyes. "Your turn."

She was surprised but she rose to the occasion. "First, likewise, my dear. Plus a good book and sunsets and gourmet chocolates," she paused, flashing a devilish grin, "and a Chippendale dancer who's just come out onto the stage. All that anticipation, you know."

"You've been to see male strippers!" he accused.

She laughed. "I was abducted. My birthday." She stepped into the hall and took his arm. "Come on. Let's go wow the Spaniard."

Sebastian, wearing a suit as black as his hair, turned away from the drinks cabinet when they entered the sitting room, arm in arm. His jaw went slack before his eyes locked with hers. She felt the heat in them from across the room.

She heard Trev ask if she wanted a drink, heard her own voice murmur, "No, thanks," but she couldn't look away. Dimly, she realized this must be how a deer feels when it was caught in someone's headlights.

Trev took a step toward the small bar then hesitated when he noticed the look on Sebastian's face and the staring match between them. "Sorry we're late," he said loudly. "I'm glad you didn't wait for us."

Sebastian dragged his gaze away from her to settle on Trev. If Trev were an insect, Sebastian would swat him with pleasure. "Good whiskey, Sinclair," he grudgingly admitted in a monotone.

Trev left her then and Sebastian closed in, one slow step at a time. "*Querida*—"

She cut him off. "Call me Ellie. Please."

"You look very beautiful and desirable tonight, Ellie." He snared her hand and lifted it toward his lips.

She gave his hand a little squeeze then pulled hers back before it reached its destination. "I have my moments, Sebastian."

From the hall, Reilly announced dinner. Sebastian, his gaze again moving over her appreciatively, held out his arm to her. She took it since there was no graceful way to ignore it. Trev, with a dark look in the direction of the hall, gave up on a drink and opened the door into the dining room for them. The look he shot Sebastian could have toasted crumpets. As they passed Trev in the doorway, she noticed a muscle working in his cheek, telling her that he was grinding his teeth.

This room delighted her as well, and she made sure Trev knew it. Here he had painted the ceiling soft rose between the delicate white curves of the fan vaulting. A huge Persian rug, its color softened by time to a warm rose, covered the hardwood floor beneath the table. The massive table, which appeared to stretch away into the shadows, and the matching high-backed chairs were of warm, aged brown wood, oak again, she guessed, as was the magnificent buffet. Finely wrought needlepoint covers on the chair seats made Ellie wonder which ancestress of Trev's had spent the necessary years with her needle to create them.

Three place settings gleamed in candlelight at one end of the table. Ellie sat on Trev's right, across the table from Sebastian.

Reilly brought in the food but they served themselves. He shot nervous glances at Sebastian before scuttling to his kitchen. Sebastian pinned him with a look, reminding her of a hawk that had just detected prey. He watched Reilly's retreat with an intensity that aroused her curiosity.

Trev and Sebastian did most of the talking, and it was tough going. Her attention was on Reilly's meal, which deserved it. A clear broth preceded a beef roast that was fork tender, accompanied by potatoes in their jackets topped with freshly churned butter, sour cream on the side, and a colorful vegetable medley. Damask cream, a milk junket flavored with rosewater and served with clotted cream, followed. Plain fare, even the Cornish pudding, but it satisfied the soul as well as the stomach. Whatever his quirks, Reilly could cook. Sebastian had done justice to Reilly's meal, too, she noticed.

"The ruins near the sea. What are they?" Sebastian asked in his thickly accented voice.

Trev's eagerness to answer probably stemmed from the dearth of conversation. She'd have to pitch in shortly.

"That's the engine house and smokestack of the abandoned Prudy's Hope tin mine."

"I don't recall seeing more of these engine houses in the area. Is the structure exclusive to this mine alone?"

"No, Prudy's Hope is the only tin mine in the immediate vicinity." Trev put down his spoon, warming to his subject.

"As the molten granite that makes up a lot of Cornwall cooled, fissures formed and other molten rocks bubbled up through them, tin, copper, zinc, lead, iron, some silver. As they cooled they formed mineral lodes. Because they formed in this way, they have to be mined vertically. Penwith sits on one of these geologic fissures, with a lode of tin beneath the ground. Cornish tin was highly prized for its purity.

"The area behind the house should be heath or meadow on this coast, but because granite underlies it and the drainage is poor, it's a kind of moor-meadow, not your usual south Cornwall sloping meadow headland or cliff. There's even a small lake. Growing up at Penwith in the midst of these things is what led me to become a geologist."

Sebastian caught her eye and sent her a smoky look. His words, however, were for Trev. "Your family was in the tin mining trade, then?"

Trev saw the look, too. Ellie busily adjusted her napkin on her lap but caught a glimpse of Trev's frown before he continued.

"Until the bottom fell out of the market. The price of tin fluctuated wildly during the seventeenth and eighteenth centuries. By the late eighteen-sixties, a third of the Cornish mining population was in America, South Africa, or Australia. There's a saying that if there's a deep hole in the ground, you'll find a Cornishman in it. Some of the tinners who remained here became wreckers, a bit of history we're not proud of, but it was the same in the north. The rest, along with the squires of Penwith, became fair-traders. Smugglers."

Sebastian set down his wine glass and leaned forward, his eyes burning. "And what of earlier times, Sinclair? I'm interested in the time of the Armada. What stories have you to tell about your ancestors who lived then?" It was a demand, not a polite request, and certainly not an attempt at conversation.

Ellie's mouth dropped open in surprise at Sebastian's rudeness. She studied the two men who watched each other, each taking the other's measure, like two dogs circling for a fight. They'd be out in the garden marking trees next. The silence dragged on. Trev was slow to answer, apparently trying to figure out what exactly this Spaniard was asking at his dinner table.

"Not many, I'm afraid," he said. "There are the usual stories about Spanish sailors washing up on the beaches, mingling with the local women, and settling here. I have some books in the library with mentions of it. Or, I could give you the name of a local historian."

"I beg your pardon but you misunderstand. Let me be direct."

Ellie nearly choked. How much more direct could Sebastian be?

He leaned back, turning his wine glass by its stem, watching Trev. "Have you heard of any jewelry pieces in local private collections that are from the Armada ships? I pay well for what I desire." His fingers stopped rotating the glass.

Trev looked at him through narrowed eyes, but before he could respond, Reilly opened the door a crack, calling Trev away from the table to take a telephone call.

Ellie felt an uneasy awareness when Sebastian's eyes and attention settled on her. Her thoughts still dwelled on his 'paying well for what he desired.'

"You are very quiet, Ellie," he said into the silence.

"And you were extremely rude just now, Sebastian." Her face probably reflected her shock when she heard herself say the words.

One hand strayed to cover her mouth.

The Spaniard looked stunned for a moment then he laughed, delighted with her show of spirit. "You are correct, I was. If you recall, I begged Sinclair's pardon at some point. Forgive me if you were bored. Armada jewelry is my passion. It is not my only passion, however." There was a wealth of innuendo in the words.

She ignored it and settled on the bored part. "I wasn't bored by your conversation. I'm still tired from my drive down here, but I could listen to Trev talk about Cornwall and Penwith all night long."

One dark, elegant eyebrow lifted into his forehead. "If I speak aloud my opinion of *talking* to a beautiful woman all night long, you would think me rude again. So, how did you meet Sinclair?" He feigned casualness but she sensed his sharp interest. He chose an apple from the fresh fruit centerpiece. It disappeared when he wrapped his big hand around it.

She told him about their letter-writing days. "As a geologist for an oil company, Trev wrote to me from all over the world. I have quite a stamp collection because of it."

With studied casualness he asked, "Did he ever write to you from South America?"

"No. He was never there, that I know of. He's been to Spain several times on holiday. Last year, he said his world-hopping days were over, perhaps permanently, and he outlined his plans for Penwith. He told me he'd taken a leave of absence, and he invited me to Penwith to help or to relax, my choice. This is my first visit."

"It took you a year to decide to come here?"

"No. I had an a-accident and couldn't come until now."

She almost continued but stopped herself in time. She didn't say that she'd had almost a year to examine her feelings for Trev. Or that spending time at Penwith meant time with him, time to get to know him in person instead of on paper, time to see if he stirred her senses as much in the flesh as he did with his written words. She didn't say any of that but glanced at the door, hoping Trev would come back or that Sebastian would drop this thread of conversation.

"And did Sinclair tell you about his family's history in his letters?" Sebastian peeled the apple with a short-bladed fruit knife. Ellie's eyes were drawn to the broad-fingered hand grasping the knife and to the apple, twirling slowly around and around in the other.

"His mother died when he was fifteen, and his father died just as he finished university. I don't think there are any other relatives. He has many good friends, though."

"Nothing about his ancestors? What about the history of Penwith itself? Did you know that Penwith was a smugglers stronghold after the family fortunes, based on tin mining, fell through?"

Ellie flinched as he cut the apple in half with one smooth motion. She sensed he was leading her relentlessly back to the unanswered question he'd put to Trev. She couldn't guess why but it was time to end it.

"I did know that, actually. I'm working on promotional materials for Penwith while I'm here. I plan to adapt both those chapters from the Sinclair family. I believe Penwith's connection with smuggling should be the main focus of all our promotion."

His eyes snagged hers. "*Our* promotion?"

This Spaniard was beginning to irritate her. "It's my way of contributing to Trev's dream. And since I'm the public relations person, may I ask how you found out about Penwith? Trev hasn't done any advertising yet."

He cut the second half of the apple into two pieces. She had the feeling he was buying time. "I believe my personal assistant found it. On the Internet, perhaps? Why do you want to know this?" His fingers stopped moving and he watched her.

The corners of her mouth lifted in a little smile of victory at irritating him in return. "Oh, I have to explore all areas of advertising to find out which are effective. Trev said you were very insistent about staying here."

He offered her a slice of apple and ate one himself before he answered. "Penwith is near Treborne, is it not? Treborne is where I will conduct some business. There must be many hiding places in this house if it was used for smuggling. Did Sinclair share any of them in his letters?"

The sneaky devil. Did he think she wouldn't notice his abrupt change of subject? He gathered what he wanted to know from anyone who might know it. They'd have to warn Reilly. And she didn't like the way Sebastian referred to Trev as 'Sinclair' all the time.

She chose her words with care. "Trev told me about the smugglers, but not about the hiding places they used," she lied. "In his letters, he talked more about the house when he considered opening parts of it for tours and renovating some of the bedrooms for a bed and breakfast operation. It's his plan to make Penwith pay for itself. I know he made an exception to accommodate you before his opening date," she told him pointedly.

Her face grew warm when he inclined his head in a tiny bow from across the table. "I will watch my manners, Ellie, have no fear. You and Sinclair will not catch me out again."

She did fear, though. And why did that sound so threatening?

She continued hurriedly. "You might be interested in some of the places Trev's work for the oil company took him. He wrote a lot about them." She went on in that vein until Sebastian's eyes glazed over and Trev came back to the table.

They returned to the sitting room where Ellie refused a snifter of brandy when Trev poured for Sebastian and himself. She accepted a cup of Reilly's freshly ground coffee and drank it standing at the French windows that overlooked the valley's march toward the sea.

"Do you smoke, Ellie?" Sebastian's voice came from behind her.

When she turned, he was standing too close. His heavy, almost feminine cologne took her breath. He flipped open the lid of an elegant box of cigarettes and offered her one.

She shook her head. "What a pretty box. Trafalgar? I've never heard of that brand."

"They are handmade for me in a little tobacconist's shop in London. I have them sent to Madrid." Light from the lamp on the table beside them played on the watered silk design stamped on glowing bronze cardboard.

She finished her coffee then excused herself when Trev left them again to meet in the library with the electrical contractor who had taken on Penwith and its tight schedule. It was his call earlier about the week's work that had taken Trev away from his dinner.

She had started up the stairs when Sebastian's voice stopped her. "I will be out later, Ellie. Will you allow me to take you for dinner and dancing one evening? Perhaps tomorrow night?"

In some strange way, this man fascinated her—and she didn't want to be fascinated by him. Every one of her senses clamored that the old adage about having a tiger by the tail definitely applied here.

She pasted a smile on her face, edging up onto the next step. "I'm not ready for night life, I'm afraid. I need a few days to settle in. And I'm not the dancer I was. The car a-accident."

"Whatever you say, Ellie. You are a beautiful and intriguing woman. I'm glad we will spend some time together here. I want very much to know you better."

He lifted her hand away from the handrail, turned it palm up this time, and placed a warm, moist kiss there. When she gasped at the sensation creeping up her arm, she saw the look of triumph in his eyes and on his face. She jerked away her arm and, feeling his gaze boring into her, she hurried up the stairs. In her room, she locked the door and shot the bolt behind her.

She washed her face and brushed her teeth in the modern bathroom that Trev had worked so hard to complete. After slipping on her silk sleep teddy and kimono, she turned to the table in front of the windows and the books from Penwith's library. She heard Sebastian's sports car roar off into the night.

A few hours of work on her laptop let her know she hadn't lied to Sebastian when she told him she was tired. She took off her kimono and sat down at the dressing table to brush her hair one hundred strokes, a habit she'd started early in life. It kept her thick hair shining and silky, saving graces in her eyes only because Trev pointed them out to her as positives.

The rumbling whisper of sound, coming from the fireplace behind her, registered in her conscious mind as the night wind whirling in the chimney. Then, without warning, there were two faces in the oval mirror. Behind hers was a specter, cobwebs draping its ears and shoulders, and a halo-like glow surrounded its oddly familiar face.

Chapter Four

ELLIE FROZE IN disbelief, accompanied by a dollop of fear. Trev had never mentioned Sinclair ghosts in Penwith. Were all Penwith spirits unique in that they carried flashlights? And did a hairbrush qualify as a deterrent against them?

It was time to find out. She raised her sturdy hairbrush in a firm grip, jumped up, and swung around to face it, prepared to administer a severe brushing if the need arose. Her bravado was spoiled by a whimper that slipped out.

When the ghost cringed, brought its hands up to protect its face, and said her name, she watched it transform into Trev. A puppet whose strings had been cut, she dropped onto the tiny dressing table chair she had just abandoned.

Trembling, she shook her hairbrush at him. "Trevor Sinclair, I will castrate you with a spoon, if you ever scare me like that again!"

"Now that's a threat I'll not take lightly!" He grinned broadly. "Sorry, Ellie. I apologize for intruding like this."

She rose to her feet when she could breathe properly. "You scared me nearly into fits. I've heard of some men being *off* the wall, Trev, but never *out* of the wall."

His eyes widened when he looked at her and a stunned look overtook his even features. "Um, it's a moving panel."

"Is it?" She crossed her arms over her chest and waited for an explanation. She tapped her foot inside its fuzzy slipper.

"In the fireplace. From the smuggling days. It swings open into a short passage that leads to stairs." His voice wasn't quite steady.

When she didn't answer, he rushed on. "The, um, stairs go down to a long passage that ends near the cliffs. My fireplace panel is on the same short passage. There's one in Reynaldos' fireplace, too, but it's blocked on the passage side. I-I wanted it to be a surprise for you."

"Oh, it was, Trev, it was." She looked at the huge gray stone now innocently back in place and masquerading as part of the back wall of the fireplace. "It must have been rough on the men in the passage if somebody built a fire smack in the middle of their escape route and the Revenue men turned up."

Her fear of total darkness, a legacy of the accident, made it difficult for her to imagine such a situation. This smugglers passage was one part of Penwith she *didn't* want to explore.

Something suddenly glinted in Trev's eyes, something deep and yearning. "But the Sinclair women always built a fire, you see, so the Revenuers wouldn't suspect should they want to search the house. Their men in the passage knew that and took their chances with being crisped around the edges."

The Revenuers might not have suspected, but she was becoming more suspicious by the moment. That was definitely a smile mixed with...whatever...in his eyes. He obviously needed prodding to loosen an explanation.

"And you felt the need to use the passage and the fireplace into my room tonight because...?"

"All will be revealed, Ellie. No pun intended." Before he looked at the ceiling, his gaze bumped down over her, and she felt its touch every place it paused.

Arms still crossed, she glanced down into her own considerable cleavage, reminding her of what she was wearing, or rather not wearing. She squealed and dove for her kimono draped across the foot of the bed. Trev turned away while she punched her arms into the wide silk sleeves.

"You can turn around now." She still felt heat in her cheeks.

"I was checking the passage for the workmen who will start in there tomorrow. I had to find out if this panel and mine still move smoothly. I apologize again for intruding on your privacy like this, but there's no way to knock on stone. And I really would like to talk with you about something."

"This panel moves smoothly. I didn't hear you or it." She stepped up to him and pinched cobwebs from his hair and shoulders.

He took a step back. "Ouch!"

"Sorry, but you're covered with them." She put her hands behind her back to stop their busy work. "Now, why do you want to talk to me?"

He turned away and ran his hands through his hair, succeeding in cobweb removal where she had failed. She knew his hair was longer than he usually wore it. Its white-gold ends curled over the edge of his shirt collar. He'd shed his jacket and tie somewhere along the way. Not, she hoped, in the dusty, cobwebby passage. His rolled-up shirtsleeves revealed well-muscled forearms sprinkled with soft golden hairs.

"Sit down, Ellie. I have something to ask you and tell you and..."

His voice faded away.

Her heart did jumping jacks. Had Trev guessed how she felt about him? Or maybe she had misread him after their kiss and it *had* affected him with its mysterious awareness. She sat down on one of the tapestry wingback chairs in front of the fireplace, demurely holding her hairbrush in her folded hands. Watching him pace the width of the room, she waited for his declaration of love.

He stopped in front of her. "What did Reynaldos talk about after I left the table tonight?"

Her hands, now clutching the hairbrush, lifted off her lap. She could still brain him with it. Given the facts, a jury of women would never convict her.

She cleared her throat and fingered the bristles instead. "He and I almost had a lively little discussion when I told him he'd been rude to you. Instead, he liked it that I stood up to him and he made nice. After that, he asked what I knew about the house and the smugglers hiding places. He wanted to know if you'd told me about them. Why?"

He turned to her. "I think Reynaldos is here to buy or to steal a family heirloom from Penwith. From me."

Her eyes opened wide. "What are you saying?"

"Do you remember the last short holiday I took to Spain not long ago, while you were still off your feet? I really went there to verify the existence of a certain sixteenth-century Spaniard. The only name I had was," he paused for effect, "Reynaldos. And an educated guess as to when he was born. I found him, Don Alonso de Reynaldos. My friend Geoff was," he paused again, a look of discomfort on his face, "tracking down someone else in Spain so he helped me find my Spaniard."

She moved to the edge of her chair. "Is Sebastian Reynaldos related to this other Reynaldos?"

"I don't know. I wasn't interested in the Don's genealogy then, just his existence, out of curiosity. I should have traced it." When she opened her mouth to speak, he held up a hand. "I'll tell you why in a minute.

"What I suspect is that if Sebastian Reynaldos turns up in the genealogy of Don Alonso de Reynaldos, then he and I are distantly related. The family connection is, er, rather tenuous."

Ellie watched him pace, admiring the easy, loose-limbed grace with which he moved. And his butt in suit pants definitely beat the Spaniard's. Hands on, er, down. Turning sharply on his heel, he caught her watching him, so she asked the first question that floated to the top of her bemused brain.

"Related? Blond-haired, blue-eyed Trevor Sinclair related to a black-haired, dark-eyed Spaniard?"

He shrugged and grinned. "The Sinclair men usually marry blondes, so they control the gene pool right now."

She played with a strand of her chestnut brown hair. It certainly wasn't blonde. "So, what heirloom do you have that Sebastian wants?"

"The sale he's going to includes sixteenth-century Spanish jewelry. He's a collector, or so he says."

Blondes? If Trev married a blonde, they'd look like twins, she mused darkly to herself. If she weren't careful she'd pout in a minute. Her lower lip itched to jut forward.

"When he was rude tonight he asked you about family stories from the time of the Spanish Armada. That's sixteenth century."

He shot her a grin. "You're quick, Ellie. He was trolling for information about Armada jewelry the whole time. When I didn't take the bait, he became more direct, if I recall."

She snorted. "Trolling with a dredge at that point." She went still for a moment as she absorbed what he had said. "And you have some jewelry from an Armada shipwreck?"

He nodded. "One piece, Ellie. One very special piece. But the story that goes with it is everything."

She pushed back in her chair, kicked off her slippers, and pulled her legs beneath her. "Tell me! I have a weakness for stories that are everything."

"And long, long legs," he muttered hoarsely. Or at least she thought that's what he said.

He glanced toward the door then dragged forward the matching chair from the opposite side of the hearth. He lowered his voice when he spoke. "I'll start at the beginning, with the facts.

"Before the first battle of the Spanish Armada, the Spanish ships anchored off the Cornish coast between the Lizard to the west of us and Plymouth to the east. On the morning of July 31, 1588, the fighting began and raged until noon. In the quiet of the afternoon, the San Salvador blew up, possibly sabotaged by one of her gunners. That was the ship our Spaniard served on, and I believe that's when he went into the water. The battle moved away eastward, up the English Channel, leaving him bobbing in the sea, at the mercy of the currents and tides.

"Now the rest of the story is oral history, the story that's been handed down through my family for generations, including the Spaniard's last name. Elizabeth Sinclair, my ancestress, was fifteen years old at the time of the Armada. She was a wild, beautiful, dark-haired girl who was learning lace making from her grandmother. She always took a shortcut along the beach to her grandmother's cottage.

"One morning, she found a half-drowned boy on the sand and shingle. His name was Reynaldos. Our research found that Don Alonso de Reynaldos was the only man by that name to serve in the Armada ranks, and that he survived to return to Spain.

"Feelings ran high during the sea battle. The villagers would have killed him if they had found him, so Elizabeth hid him in a secret cave and took food, blankets, and clothing to him. The boy didn't speak English and Elizabeth didn't speak Spanish, but they understood each other from the first moment."

Trev's tone changed, becoming softer, more intimate. He spent time with each word, savoring it before he let it go. "They were perfect strangers who were perfect for each other. They fell deeply in love and..." His voice slid to a halt as their gazes locked.

Sharing that utterly still, utterly aware moment with him, Ellie felt a breathless, fluttering excitement from the tips of her fingers to the tips of her toes.

He cleared his throat and continued. "After things calmed down, other survivors remained here, fathered families, and lived out their lives. But Elizabeth understood that her Spaniard yearned for Spain. In a supreme act of unselfishness, she made arrangements through one of her seafaring brothers for him to return to his homeland. He wanted her to go with him, but she refused. On the night he left, he gave to her the jeweled cross he wore around his neck. He also gave her a son.

"The Spaniard's cross and the young lovers' story have been passed down from generation to generation in my family since that night. And I think the Spaniard's cross is why Reynaldos is here."

Ellie dashed the tears from her eyes. "What a beautiful love story. And you have the Spaniard's cross? Here at Penwith?"

"Safe and sound in a smugglers hiding place in my room."

Her tears dried and excitement took over. "And Sebastian was asking about hiding places in Penwith!"

He stood up, holding out his hand to her. Without thinking, she nestled her palm against his. He pulled her to her feet.

His next words held the eagerness of a little boy with secrets and treasures to share. "I'll show you the cross, but first let me demonstrate how the secret panel works."

When she protested and held back, he tugged her forward. Surely, for Trev's sake, she could handle looking into an old tunnel from the warmth, light, and safety of this lovely room, especially with him at her side.

The massive panel operated on a simple balance system. By pressing the flat of his hand against the rectangular stone's upper right hand corner and pushing firmly, Trev swung the heavy slab open into the pitch-black passage behind it.

She was mistaken. In an instant she was smothering, suffocating in the cool fresh air, smelling of moor and sea, which moved over her and around her. Her gasp expelled the remaining air from her lungs and left her unable to take in more. Doing a great imitation of a poorly constructed house of cards, her knees gave way beneath her. A look of dismay sped across Trev's features. He caught her in his arms and sat down with her on the chair he'd just taken her from.

He held her against him, fanning air into her face with his free hand. "Ellie! Ellie, dar—! Ellie, what is it?"

She strained to breathe over the panic. At the hospital, she had been taught to visualize something or somewhere pleasant. Often she chose Penwith, but Trev's face so close to hers did nicely and she fixed her attention on him. But her glimpse of the velvety blackness behind the stone played over and over again in her mind, clinging and fading reluctantly.

Finally, she was able to speak. "Total darkness. From the a-accident. I was trapped...in the dark until a truck driver came with a flashlight. His name was Chance."

Trev's breath came out in a rush. "Oh, Ellie, I didn't realize it was like that. But I didn't want to take you inside, just to show you how it operates. I'm so sorry."

He rocked her with his body movement and patted her back until she went limp and breathed normally again. "You know you can talk to me about this, about anything, when you're ready?"

She nodded. "I know. And I will. J-Just not yet. Okay?"

"All right. I'll show you the cross another time."

"No, you will not!" she heard herself say, surprising both of them. "After hearing that beautiful story, I want to see it now. Besides, I think it will help me sleep. Take my mind off... That or a stiff drink but not the pills."

She felt his smile rather than saw it. "Good. And we'll go by way of the hall. Ready?"

At her nod, he set her on her feet and led her to the door. When she tried to explain why she'd locked it, he interrupted, saying, "No, it's a good idea, when our little family isn't alone in the house," making her almost purr with contentment.

His room was next to hers, putting her in an interesting position. She was sandwiched between an Englishman of Don Alonso de Reynaldos' descent on one side of her, and a Spaniard of the same busy Don's descent on the other.

In the light from a lone lamp on Trev's desk, she got the impression of beautiful, ancient, heavy wood furniture. A spicy, masculine scent hung in the air, a mixture of leather, books, fresh air, and moor flowers. Again, the stone cavern of the fireplace was big enough for Ellie to stand in.

"Here, under the edge of the mantel near the wall, is a hollowed out hiding place. Do you remember my telling you about it?" As Trev spoke, he withdrew from it a burgundy velvet pouch with a drawstring.

He took her hand and led her over to the desk, adjusting the lamp's shade until it spotlighted an area on the blotter. Then he tipped the pouch's contents into the beam's center.

An intricately carved three-inch-long gold cross on a sturdy gold chain slid out in a tangled, glowing heap. Single intersecting rows of glowing red stones caught the light, creating a fiery cross within a cross. Ellie's little whistle of amazement turned into a gasp of disbelief followed by a low moan of pleasure.

She looked to Trev for permission then picked it up, letting the cross rest against her palm as the chain dangled from her fingers. Its red fire dazzled her. Seven stones, three round, one oval, two square, and one pear-shaped, burned with an otherworldly light against the warm highlights of the gold.

"It's solid gold," she whispered. "And are these stones...?"

"Rubies." Trev dug in his desk drawer and handed her a magnifying glass. "Here, try this."

Through it, the details of the cross leaped out at her. "See how rough the carving is, and the stones are cabochons, highly polished but not faceted." Her voice dropped to a whisper. "And look at the chain! Each link is handcrafted."

They were cheek to cheek, his light hair mingling with her dark as he joined her in peering through the large lens. Ellie grew silent as the length of chain flowed across her fingers beneath the glass. It was wondrously worked with tiny flower-shaped disks decorating each link.

"Here, try it on." Even as she protested, he slid the chain over her head

Its weight, and especially its unexpected warmth, surprised her, since its hiding place had been cold stone. She laid a hand on it and felt her heartbeat through its familiar shape. She turned, searching for a mirror, and went to the only one, hanging above Trev's bureau.

The Spaniard's cross looked out of place against the v-neck of her kimono. So, she tugged at the wrap's tie and opened it. She lifted her heavy hair from the back of her neck with one hand and took up a loop of chain in the other so that the gold of the cross rested against her skin, just above her silk-covered breasts.

Trev's quiet voice came from behind her. "I've always wondered what it would look like against a long white throat and soft shoulders."

Wrapped in her own experience and pleased that it looked so good against her skin, she continued for him. "Or above a gown of rich silk and fine lace? Or against thick, jewel-hued velvet?"

She sensed the heat of passion and love in its glowing gold and fiery stones, yet there was an aura of sadness about it, too. Elizabeth and her Spaniard had parted. Maybe history would repeat itself. When it came time for her to leave Penwith, would Trev let her go, merely seeing off a friend who was heading back home, feeling nothing more?

She pushed back those thoughts and concentrated on the feelings generated by the cross. Her eyes were drawn to the fireplace, reflected in the mirror. There, in imaginary flames, she saw another fire lighting craggy stone walls and the faces of a dark-haired boy and girl. As the boy leaned forward to take the girl in his arms, the cross around his neck swung forward on its chain. The precious metal and fiery stones caught the light and burned like their love.

Trev's amused voice jolted her back to reality. "I take it you approve?"

She sighed and turned to him, letting go of her hair and the chain. "I approve. No wonder Sebastian wants it."

Trev's gaze took a slow journey from the cross against the silk to her face. "He's never seen it. Nobody has, except family. We've never shown it or allowed it to be photographed."

Excitement bubbled up within her as an idea took shape in her mind. "Trev, if you displayed the cross here, at Penwith, and published the story of Elizabeth and her Spaniard, you'd have to beat people away from your door."

He shook his head. "It's too private. There's a very personal family tradition that involves the cross. I'll tell you about it, when the time is right."

"You're the boss." She lifted the chain over her head and reluctantly handed the cross to him. "And Sebastian hasn't asked you about it? Directly, I mean."

Trev studied the cross, frowning. "Not yet, but it's coming. I wonder how he found out about it?"

She retied her wrap. "The Spaniard lived, returned to Spain, and certainly married there. The Spanish side of the family might have a story about the cross, too. Maybe you and Sebastian have worked steadily toward each other by doing research on a shared family legend."

"I hadn't thought of that. I'm glad you're here to give me new perspective on this."

She almost purred again under his warm approval. "He was vague about how he found Penwith, by the way. 'Perhaps his personal assistant found it on the Internet,' that kind of thing. Do you have a web site or a homepage, or have you listed with any travel sites on the Internet?"

"No to all of the above."

"I handled things like that for the library, and I can do it for Penwith, when you're ready for floods of reservations. And I'll try to find out more from Sebastian, even though his touch gives me chills."

She had been watching the muscles ripple across the width of Trev's shoulders beneath his white shirt as he put the cross back into its hiding place. Now, his back abruptly stiffened.

"Reynaldos touched you?" he asked tonelessly, turning to look at her.

She shrugged, trying to make light of it, although she shivered. "He kissed my hand. Twice. Once on the back, once on the palm. You were there for the first one."

"And the second?"

She cleared her throat and looked at him, the memory in her eyes. "Tonight, as I was coming up the stairs to my room."

"And then you locked your door. The predatory bastard," he muttered.

She felt a frisson of pleasure at his tone. "Trev, I think I can sleep now, without the pills. Thank you for showing me the cross. Are you sure it's safe there?"

"It's been safe there for over four hundred years. Shall I see you safely back to your room?"

She moved toward the door. "No, it's only a few steps. I'll scream if I need help."

A moment later, she wished she *had* allowed him to at least watch while she walked back to her room. Because she ran smack into Sebastian Reynaldos two steps outside Trev's door.

Chapter Five

SEBASTIAN'S WARM, APPRAISING gaze leisurely moved from her disheveled head to her fuzzy-slippered feet, pausing on the cleavage that showed above her hastily tied kimono.

"Good evening, Ellie," he said calmly. "You reconsidered your early night?"

Her face erupted in a scorching blush as she inched sideways along the wall toward her door. "Oh. I...Hello, Sebastian. You're back early. Trev and I were just...going over tomorrow's schedule."

"I see. And what *is* tomorrow's schedule?" There was amusement in his eyes as he kept pace with her progress along the wall.

"Um, Trev is taking the Land Rover for service tomorrow morning before he joins the workmen in the left wing." It wasn't a lie. Trev had mentioned at dinner that he had an appointment for the Rover at Avallen's lone garage tomorrow. "I told him I'd walk in and meet him. I'd like to see the church. And I'm supposed to walk. Doctor's orders." She bumped into a table.

Sebastian took advantage of the obstacle and moved closer to her. "If you don't wish to sleep, Ellie, I am available for anything else you have in mind. Or desire." He reached out to feel a strand of her hair, much as Trev had done the night before on the sofa. "I promise you won't be disappointed." His voice was silky on the last words.

Her knees sagged for just a moment before she pushed herself against the wall. For some incomprehensible reason, words of attraction and invitation from this man were heady stuff, but not heady enough to quiet her intuition. Some woman part of her sensed that Sebastian's lovemaking would be equal measures of heat and chill, treading a thin line between pleasure and pain. Now if those same words had issued from Trev's lips, she wouldn't have had a prayer or a moment's hesitation.

She covered her momentary lapse with a smile and a direct approach. "I'm sure you're, er, very good...at what you do, Sebastian. But don't you think you're rushing things when we've known each other less than a day?"

He put one hand on the wall on each side of her. When she jerked back, her head smacked against the wood panels.

"Of what importance is time? I've noticed you are not indifferent to me, Ellie. When a Spaniard's blood is up, it is as hot as our sultry climate. Time means nothing."

Trev's door jerked open a few yards to her right, and he shot out into the hall. His shirt flapped, gaping wide. His hair was mussed, and he was barefoot. Her mouth dropped open in shock before she recovered and shot him a look of amazement. He wanted Sebastian to think they had...?

"Ellie! Glad I caught you." She realized his teeth were clenched, more bared than smiling. Especially telling was the word 'caught.' "You forgot your notes."

Sebastian stepped back and, thoroughly shaken, she took the folded paper Trev held out to her. "Thank you. I'm going to bed now. Good night."

She shuffled along what seemed an unnaturally long length of hall to her own door, swearing to herself with every step that she was giving up fuzzy slippers for the rest of her life. Her hand on the knob, she turned to see two appraising stares directed at her legs, exposed from just above the knee where her kimono ended to her ankles, where the fuzzy slippers took over. At least her surgery scars weren't on view. She swallowed a scream when a black shadow shot between her feet and into the room ahead of her. Traveller calmly curled up in her place on the coverlet at the foot of the bed while Ellie nearly gibbered with nerves.

"I wish to speak to you, Sinclair," she heard Sebastian say before she slammed her door. Trev, ever polite, invited him to the library for a nightcap and a chat.

She leaned against the door after sliding the bolt home. What if Sebastian had listened at Trev's door? She had been moving toward it when she asked Trev about the safety of the cross's hiding place. She turned to touch the wood panels behind her. These old doors were thick but were they thick enough against determination?

She'd love to find out. Holding a glass to the library door crossed her mind. She would pay money to know what was being said in there at that moment. Instead, she unfolded the paper clutched in her hand. One giant exclamation point filled the page and brought a smile to her face. The smile was still in place when she sank into the comfortable bed and gave herself up to sleep.

TRAVELLER, GIVING a great impression of a cat whose tail was being wound up in a winch, woke her in good time the next morning. She showered, dressed for comfort, and went down the back stairs to the kitchen. Trev was drinking coffee and finishing a stack of pancakes at the table. Out in the hall, the Hoover hummed under Annie's guidance. What riveted her attention, however, was Reilly, rolling out dough with quick, sharp movements.

"I thought you would sleep awhile this morning," Trev said by way of greeting.

"I thought I would, too, especially after that incident outside your door last night. Do you think Sebastian heard what we were talking about?"

She couldn't help herself. Her gaze slid away from Trev to Reilly. Dough fascinated her, since her own modest attempts with it were usually followed by long sessions with a vacuum cleaner, followed by vigorous application of a kitchen knife to the bottoms of her shoes to scrape off the dough she stepped in.

She went to where Reilly worked and leaned against the countertop beside him. Should a pane of glass magically appear between them, her nose would be pressed against it in wonder.

"You make that look so easy. What are you making?" Her voice reflected her awe, and she told him about her adventures with dough.

Reilly laughed at her stories and appeared pleased by her interest and admiration. "These are Cornish pasties for dinner tonight."

She watched, fascinated, as he folded a short crust over chopped meat, onion, and potatoes to make a kind of turnover. "I've never tasted a pasty but I've read about them in an old Cornish recipe book I found at a used book store back home."

Trev joined her at the counter, leaning beside and behind her, folding his long body slightly around hers. "They were a portable lunch for the working men of Cornwall. A pasty was easy to carry and could have savory at one end and sweet at the other."

Reilly used a sharp knife to cut one initial, 'E,' 'T,' 'R,' 'A,' and 'S,' into the dough in the corners of five pasties.

Before she asked, Trev explained. "Reilly makes pasties in the old way. They were marked with initials. The miners and fishermen began eating their pasties at the opposite corner so that if their meal was interrupted, the owner would know which pasty was his when he got back to it."

Delighted with the information, she allowed Trev to lead her to the table where she helped herself to pancakes, bacon, and coffee. "Well, do you think Sebastian heard anything through the door?"

Trev frowned. "I had to crack my door before I could hear clearly what you two were saying in the hall. And we were speaking in normal to lower tones, weren't we, and well across the room? By the way, he's *heard* about an Armada cross at Penwith, although he won't come right out and say he knows my family's legend."

She stopped stirring her coffee. "And that's what he wanted to talk to you about last night?"

Trev nodded then grimaced. "It was a beautiful dance. He made me an offer for this phantom cross but wouldn't tell me where he heard about it. I wouldn't admit there was a cross. I wonder if the information came from Geoff. Or indirectly from Geoff."

Reilly dropped a small pan just then, making her jump. Trev watched him closely as Reilly said, "Sorry, guv."

"Geoff is the friend you're expecting? But why indirectly?"

"He lives in Spain and I stayed with him while I was there. I told him a little about the cross when he helped me verify there was a Spaniard named Reynaldos who sailed with the Armada and survived. He knew I wasn't interested in the modern Reynaldos clan, just the old Spaniard's existence. Now, I wonder if Geoff stopped looking when I did.

"Also, Geoff has a girlfriend I don't trust, Inez Concepcion. I'd suspect her of giving the information to Sebastian before I'd suspect Geoff. I think it's time to contact my old mate to find out what he's been up to and when he's coming here."

"Sounds like a good idea."

He pushed back his chair. "So, are you coming into Avallen with me? We can drop the Rover at the garage and do a little exploring before I have to get back. Or, we can talk to more business owners about group advertising."

She jumped at the chance to go, but she opted to see the church first, with him, then stay in town alone to talk to the business owners he'd introduced her to yesterday. Her walk back to Penwith would be her exercise for the day.

Penwith's vehicle was a venerable Land Rover, which she checked out as she climbed inside. It had been lovingly cared for. The engine purred and the interior was spotlessly clean.

"This would do very well to transport guests and their luggage to or from the train station. For special cases and circumstances only, of course. But it's another service we—you—can offer."

Trev's driving passed her inspection, too. Having used the cliff road all his life, he appeared to know it well. His braking and gearing were down to a fine art. His confidence resulted in more speed than she would have liked, however.

"Now, tell me the gory details," she said after a while. "How did Sebastian bring up the subject of the cross and what did you say to him?"

"He started the moment the library door closed behind us. He said he'd heard a story, from someone who knows he collects Armada jewelry, that there was an Armada cross at a house called Penwith in Cornwall, England. At no point did I admit I had a cross. But, I said, if there *was* a cross, that meant it would be over four hundred years old and a family heirloom."

She watched his profile and decided to risk one rude question. "May I ask what he offered for it?"

He grimaced. "A blank check, which I could certainly use. My answer to that was, if there *was* a family heirloom cross, did he really expect me to sell it to him?"

"I'll bet he didn't take that well. He reminds me of the president of our library board of directors, quietly dangerous when crossed."

"At first I thought he took it calmly enough, then as you said, not well at all. He couldn't hide the cold, threatening anger in his voice and manner. By the time he stormed out of the room, I sensed he had iron determination to find the cross."

"And you think your friend Geoff's girlfriend might be the leak?"

"Inez. Geoff's a good friend, a nomad who has fallen on hard times. We're old school chums. He was shot—"

Her head jerked around in his direction when he abruptly stopped speaking. Pain showed in the grimace on his face. She wondered what had happened to his friend and waited quietly for him to tell her what it was.

"Geoff was...injured, overseas, while on rotation off the North Sea oil platforms. Because of constant pain, he was unable to perform his duties and he lost his job. He moved to Spain for several reasons, including the climate. I invited him to stay at Penwith this spring and summer in exchange for help in the gardens. He said he would take me up on it this month. I e-mailed him this morning, asking what's going on."

They were negotiating a series of sharp curves on the cliff road now and she wondered why Trev didn't slow down. When she turned to ask him, the words stalled in her throat. His face was pasty white.

"Bloody hell!" The words were half-shout, half-moan as he geared down and fought the steering wheel on a curve.

From her movie viewing and book reading experiences, she knew it wasn't good when a driver reacted this way. "What's wrong?"

"No bloody brakes!" He shifted down again and hauled back on the emergency brake.

But it wasn't enough and it came too late.

Other than a moment of her heart cowering in the vicinity of first her throat then her navel, she didn't have time to be frightened. There was a brief, sickening view of sky and sea and surf breaking on black rocks below as they slid, in slow motion, through the wooden fence and over the edge of the cliff on the next curve.

She braced herself with her left hand on the dash while the right reached out to Trev. So, she was meant to die here, a year later, in Cornwall's clear light and with Trev beside her, instead of alone in the dark an ocean's width away. For that she was grateful.

She expected the Rover to begin a death roll, end over end. It didn't. She expected pain. There wasn't any. She expected them to be dead. They weren't. She opened her eyes and looked around a few seconds after they stopped moving.

Maybe the ghosts of Trev's ancestors who had lived and worked and smuggled along these cliffs had looked out for them in their moment of peril. On this particular curve, the cliff was stepped. A wide, flat dirt and rock ledge projected out from the face. The Land Rover had plonked onto it, upright, but with a bone-jarring jolt, like it had planned the whole thing.

A heavy silence followed. Even the sea birds stilled their raucous cries, probably in amazement, at the acrobatics of the green metal box with windows, and the two floppy humans who quaked within it.

Ellie turned her head to stare out her side window at the sheer drop and the jagged rocks below, awash with white sea foam. Then, from somewhere, a keening mantra began, "Ohmygod, ohmygod, ohmygod..." Ellie wondered where it came from until Trev pulled her around to face him and shook her. The sound stopped abruptly.

"Out my side. Now!" When she didn't move, he reached across her and unfastened her seat belt, pulling her toward him.

Instantly she understood his urgency. The dirt ledge, soaked by the recent rains, might give way beneath the weight of the Land Rover. Nothing got by her for long these days, especially the fact that her life had just been spared a second time in the span of twelve months.

Trev eased open his door until it touched the dirt face then pulled her over onto his lap. Holding onto each other, they rolled, slid, fell out, landing in a heap on the ledge between the Land Rover and the face. Not moving, they waited for the descending elevator feeling to begin, should they, their trusty vehicle, and a hunk of Cornwall real estate continue the journey into the English Channel.

Their positions were reversed from their first meeting. She lay on top of him, nose to nose this time. Staring into Trev's eyes, she saw her own parade of emotions reflected there—first horror, followed by hope, finally relief, then something else—a hunger with a sharp and feral edge.

In the next second, Trev wound his fingers into her hair and pulled her down to meet his lips. Her helpless shiver of desire communicated itself to him and she felt him tremble in response. They might yet die on those rocks down there and she would not let this opportunity, possibly her last chance in this life to kiss him, pass her by. And so, taking a firm grip on *his* hair, she devoured, ruthlessly plundered, sampled, and hoarded his kiss until she was sure she could put a Sinclair smuggler to shame.

When she finally pulled back and looked at him, he wore his familiar, dazed look. "Sorry, Ellie," he said hoarsely. "Adrenaline high."

"Likewise, my dear," she panted.

Trev levered her to her feet then pushed himself up and moved to the rear of the vehicle. He opened the back an inch at a time and took out a rope.

A smallish boulder jutted out from the face at the edge of the ledge. He helped her onto it. "Sit tight. Quietly tight," he amended. "I'll climb up then throw the rope down to you. Unless you want to climb—"

She gave one violent shake of her head, unable to speak, afraid to move any other part of her body.

He shrugged the coil of rope over his neck and one shoulder then started to climb. She watched, her own neck protesting its odd angle. He went with care, feeling for footholds and handholds before transferring his weight, until he reached the top.

She turned back to the ledge, massaging her neck. Something caught her eye, glinting in the sunlight in the dirt where the back fender had gouged the cliff face. The object was within reach from her perch. She recognized it immediately. Its presence there, where it had no right to be, was accompanied by a new twist of fear in her gut. Leaning sideways, she picked up the article with two fingers and pushed it into her jacket pocket.

Trev secured the rope to something she couldn't see. He made a noose in the loose end, threw it down to her, and told her how and where to put it around her body. She did so without leaving her seat. Then she stood up on her boulder and he pulled her up to him, with her help when she could find purchase with her feet or hands. After he hauled her over the edge, she threw herself into his arms. They simply held each other.

His voice was ragged when he spoke. "Are you hurt?"

"No. Just s-shook up."

"Let's sit down for a minute."

She was up for that. Her body folded down on itself, right where she stood, resembling a soufflé she'd once made.

Trev plopped down beside her. "We're halfway between the house and Avallen. I'd like to head for Avallen and the garage. Jock has a tow truck. Maybe we can save the Rover."

She nodded. "I can do Avallen. In a minute."

He wiped the gleam of perspiration from his forehead. "It's times like this I wish I smoked."

That reminded her of what was in her windbreaker pocket. "Trev, why were you taking the Rover in for service today?"

"It wasn't for brakes, if that's what you're thinking. It had a full brake system replacement not long ago. It was scheduled for regular maintenance service today. I think you would call it a lube and an oil change."

"It's funny you should mention smoking." She reached into her pocket and showed him what she'd found, telling him where she'd found it.

It was a wide, slim box. Trafalgar Cigarettes was stamped in fancy black letters on the bronze watered-silk design cardboard. She flipped open the top with her thumb. A line of cigarettes marched across the opening.

"They're specially made for Sebastian Reynaldos in London. Has he been anywhere near the Rover when he could have left this?"

Trev took the box and studied it. "He asked to see the engine yesterday. He was smoking and blowing it right into my face until we put our heads under the bonnet. But I saw him put the box into his pocket."

"Maybe he did, that time," she suggested softly.

His eyes narrowed when he looked at her. "The crazy bastard," he whispered.

She agreed.

Chapter Six

THEY WALKED OFF some of their reaction on the way to Jock Polwarren's garage in Avallen. Trev took the owner aside and told him what had happened and that they suspected tampering. Then he delivered her to a teashop and arranged for a steady supply of hot, sweet tea, teacakes, and biscuits before he climbed up into his seat beside Jock in the tow truck.

She was awash with tea, sated with sweets, and wallowing in suppositions by the time he returned. His face was grim, his words even more grim.

"Jock says the brake line *might* have been tampered with. He found a tiny hole in it, maybe deliberate, maybe by accident. If it was done on purpose then it was so cleverly done that he can't be positive."

"And we can't prove a thing."

She had avoided thinking about their kiss until that moment. Trev had attributed their first kiss to exhaustion and this kiss to an adrenaline high. She wondered if he would ever kiss her, pull back, look deep into her eyes, and say, "No apologies, Ellie, because that was pure, unadulterated love and lust on my part, and I fully intend to continue in the same vein." Her face grew warm at the thought.

Trev didn't notice, staring into his teacup. "Jock can be very discreet. I've asked him to keep this to himself for the time being."

She brought her mind to bear on the business at hand. "Wouldn't you notice drips or puddles where the Rover sits if it was a slow, simple, accidental leak?"

"You're right, I would and I didn't. That means the fluid was collected in something. The line could have been disconnected and drained until just enough remained to allow the brakes to work properly for a bit, then the hole made to finish the job when I applied the brakes. I haven't used it since I got back from Treborne the night you arrived. That indicates it was done after that. And the Rover is too old to have warning lights for system failures. Reynaldos asked me its model year."

They looked at each other and silently acknowledged their gut feeling that their accident had not been accidental. Suspecting was one thing, knowing they were right was quite another. They both had more hot, sweet tea, teacakes, and biscuits before they continued.

Trev fired the opening volley. "Why would Reynaldos want the Spaniard's cross so much that he'd do something like this?"

She was ready. "I made good use of the time I spent gulping tea, and I have a few 'maybes' to toss out. I don't read thrillers for naught. One, maybe Sebastian *is* simply the ultimate, obsessed collector. Maybe he'll do anything to possess something as beautiful as the Spaniard's cross, even sight unseen, especially if he's related to Don Alonso de Reynaldos and thinks it rightfully belongs to him."

"You *have* been thinking over your tea, haven't you? With me dead, though, he stands very little chance of getting the cross. Based on what I saw of his behavior last night in the library, I can believe your theory, up to a point. And after today's contribution, I can also believe he's simply barking mad—and that's throwing roses at him. You said 'maybes'?"

She hesitated. "Maybe it's what owning the cross signifies to the world that's important rather than the cross itself."

He tore his attention away from his teacup and cocked his head to look at her. "Such as?"

In a whisper she dropped her bomb into the clatter and chatter of the busy teashop. "What if Elizabeth Sinclair and Don Alsonso de Reynaldos were married before he went back to Spain? What if the cross symbolizes that marriage?"

His head jerked up, he opened his mouth to speak, then closed it again. "Our family is small," he said, hesitating. "We've never reproduced in large numbers, so the family legend is a particularly quiet one, as legends go. If any of my ancestors bothered to find out or were successful, that fact would have been passed down with the rest of the story. But what brought Reynaldos haring to England to reclaim the cross now?"

"Ah, that would be 'maybe' number three. Maybe there's a clock ticking somewhere in Sebastian's life, a reason he thinks he has to have the cross now. Something we don't know. You could ask Geoff to scope out this modern-day Spaniard, if he hasn't already."

He nodded slowly. "I like the wedding theory, Ellie. There has always been something missing from their story, Elizabeth and her Spaniard. Their love reaches down through the ages in the cross. I can feel it when I touch it. And yet..."

Then what she felt when she touched the cross wasn't her imagination because Trev felt it, too. "And to find out if we're right, we would look... Where would we look, Trev?"

He thought for a moment. "Of course! The parish records at St. Matthew's Church. Over four hundred years have passed, though. Maybe they're gone." Then his eyes lit up and he grinned at her. "There's one way to find out. If you've finished sipping tea, Ellie Jaymes, let me show you our church."

She was sure she sloshed when she stood up. After a bathroom visit, she was ready.

When they stepped out into the sunlight and looked up, the gray-black, weathered stone square tower of St. Matthew's served as a backdrop to the cottage rooftops, situated as it was on a slight rise at the edge of the village proper. They walked up a narrow, winding paved path to get to the little church. The only other route was across a field. Ellie commented on the strangeness of the approach.

"The restricted access came about because of the plague," Trev explained. "When the old village was devastated by the epidemic, it was abandoned and a new village was built on this side of the church. The field over there is where the old village once stood. This path continues around to the proper church entry."

Trev opened the heavy wooden door, and they stepped into cool half-light. Dark red runners of carpet crossed each other at the transept of the shiny stone-flagged aisles and muffled their footsteps. Ceiling arches of stone soared above the tall ends of the carved wooden pews. The windowsills were a foot deep.

"There's a list of vicars at St. Matthew's dating from the year thirteen-twenty," Trev told her softly. "I believe there's a Sinclair on it from around the time of the Armada."

"I have no problem imagining a clandestine wedding here," she whispered.

She could almost hear the vows of Elizabeth Sinclair and Don Alonso de Reynaldos echo off the stones, returning to marry the couple a second and third time. It would have given the ceremony a dreamlike quality.

Near the altar, a woman in a flowered smock was on her knees polishing the wooden railing. She stood up and came toward them with quick, bouncy steps. Trev introduced Ellie to Ruth Littledale, the vicar's wife.

"Grant is in Penzance today. He'll be sorry he missed you," she bubbled while she pumped Ellie's hand. "If you'll be with us for a while, you must come to services and to Sunday dinner. Would you like to step over to the vicarage now for a cup of tea?"

They both spoke up when the flow of words stopped. Ellie

declared she couldn't hold another cup of tea at the moment but would like to accept Ruth's invitation soon. Trev got down to business.

"Another time, thank you, Ruth. I wonder if you can help us? We'd like to see the parish records for 1588 and 1589."

"Ah, you want the record books in the case up in the tower." She led the way up flights of stairs that became narrower and steeper as they went. "It's surprisingly dry up here, so the books are in good condition, despite their age. You have to be very careful, though, because the pages are delicate. But I know I can trust you, Trevor."

She left them in a tiny room under the bell chamber in the tower. A dozen or more volumes of parish records lay in a glass-fronted cupboard. Trev lifted out the one that included the years 1588 and 1589.

"What date should we start looking under?" he asked, placing the book carefully on a wooden table against the wall.

Ellie sat in the only chair. She reached up and turned on the ancient metal desk lamp that would be their source of light. "Let's see. You said the Spaniard went into the water on July 31, 1588? Then I'd say we should start looking for a marriage in early October or November, but we should scan everything from the beginning of August anyway, for any mention of Armada survivors."

The only Spaniards mentioned were those who didn't survive and who were buried in a corner of the churchyard outside. The others were simply absorbed into the society of 16th-century Cornwall, thanks to the Cornish women who lived then. She wondered what special stories other local families might tell about Armada survivors in their family trees.

Pieces of brittle parchment flaked between some of the pages. The first pages for the month of October were in good condition and appeared, judging by the number of entries in faded ink, to have been busy.

It was easy for Ellie to get caught up in the fascinating social history of Avallen in the 16th century. She paused often to read aloud to Trev the entries that caught her eye. He urged her onward.

She turned a page to find a section littered with tiny pieces of parchment, some of which fluttered to the floor. "This page has completely disintegrated." She paused, puzzled. "But the edge is perfect and still bound tightly into the spine," she added, tugging on it gently.

She examined the pages on either side of the debris. "Some of October fourteenth, all of October fifteenth, and some of October sixteenth, fifteen-eighty-eight, are gone."

They scanned the entries for a full twelve months, the period that would cover the birth and baptism of a child, if the Sinclair family legend was true. They found nothing except another disintegrated page for a date in July and another in August of 1589.

Mrs. Littledale stirred from her work when they plodded down from the tower, quietly discussing what they might try next.

"Did you find what you were looking for?" she asked cheerfully.

Trev's disappointment showed on his face. "A few of the pages have disintegrated, Ruth. If the entries we're looking for were on those pages, then we have no way of finding them."

Mrs. Littledale twisted her polishing cloth in her hands and looked away. "I didn't tell the other gentleman this, Trevor, but you can check the missing pages at St. Luke's in Treborne. The parish records were microfilmed in the 1970s and sent there for safekeeping. Since then, I believe, they've been updated and might even be on a computer."

Ellie felt relief and excitement at Ruth's words, until she sensed Trev's sudden stillness. When he spoke, his quiet, authoritative tone made her straighten.

"What other gentleman, Ruth?"

Ruth Littledale continued twisting the cloth but met Trev's intense gaze, a small animal caught hopelessly in his headlights. "A foreign gentleman came in about a week ago and asked to see the parish records. I took him up to the tower and insisted on staying with him, because I didn't know him, you see. He didn't like it, I can tell you.

"Then Mrs. Grenville came in to do the flowers for the altar, and I had to leave him for a few minutes. I met him on the tower stairs as I was starting back up. He said he couldn't find what he was looking for and that some of the pages were crumbled. He seemed very satisfied about the whole thing. I didn't tell him about St. Luke's because... Well, I didn't like his attitude. Grant wasn't happy with me when I told him what I'd done."

Ellie jumped into the tiny gap when Mrs. Littledale paused to breathe. "What did he look like, Mrs. Littledale?"

"Big, tanned, tailored suit, and lots of gold jewelry. Handsome devil." She stopped, excitement heavy in her words. "But you know him. I heard that he's staying at Penwith. Oh, I hope I didn't—"

Trev's hand tightened on Ellie's arm before he interrupted. "You did the right thing, Ruth. Ellie and I will explain it all to you and Grant some time. Thank you for your help. I'll bring Ellie around again," he said as he pulled her toward the door.

"Sebastian," she hissed when they once again stood in the sunshine. "He was in the area a week before he came to Penwith."

Trev nodded, taking her hand and moving away from the church. "Who else? He could have done my brake line any time he bloody well chose."

She didn't jump to that conclusion. "Without trying to get the cross first? I'll bet he did your brakes last night, Trev, after your little chat in the library. It makes more sense that he'd wait until after he offered for it. He didn't know you'd turn him down, especially if local gossip says money is tight at Penwith. The man doesn't waste any time."

"You're right, of course, it's no secret. I was born and raised here, but it's human nature to speculate whether or not I'll fall on my face. I'll bet those pages were just fine before Ruth Littledale left Reynaldos alone with them." His tone was ominous.

"They were okay up to the page with some of October 14, all of October 15, and part of October 16 on it." She counted nine months on her fingers. "The missing page in July could be the baby's birth and the August one could be the entry for the baby's baptism. The timing is right. We'll have to go to St. Luke's in Treborne. When?"

"Soon. I can't get away for the next day or so until I know Geoff's schedule. And the work is picking up. As much as I hate to suggest this, I think a thorough look around Reynaldos' room might be in order in the meantime. Maybe he took notes before he destroyed the pages, or maybe he tore them out."

When she thought about Sebastian walking in on Trev, a stab of fear replaced her initial surprise at his suggestion. "When is this sale Sebastian says he's attending? Have you checked to see if there *is* a sale?"

"Oh, the sale is legitimate, all right. The preview is tomorrow. The sale is the following day. Why?"

"Because the safest time to search his room is when you're sure he's out of the way for a while. If I go with him, I can make sure he stays away from Penwith. While I keep him occupied, you can take your time and put everything back in its place."

His eyes narrowed suspiciously. "Occupied?"

She disregarded the single word with its payload of meaning. Concentrating on Trev's safety, she tried to ignore his dislike of Sebastian and her own reactions to the Spaniard.

"Sebastian likes me. You said so yourself. And then there's the hand kissing. I'll make sure he stays away from the house while you look through his things. If he tries to come back early, I'll say my leg is bothering me to slow us down. I'll be fine if I deny any knowledge of a cross or a family legend or hiding places in Penwith."

Trev harrumphed, her second harrumph since she'd come to Penwith. "He appeared to want more than hand kissing last night."

"That was just his knee-jerk reaction to the situation."

"Really? Were his knees involved as well?"

She glanced at him. "I've been meaning to ask. I know what I looked like when I came out of your room, but why did you...look the way you did when you came flying out your door, like you'd just been kissed senseless?"

"It was a ploy to protect you. My reasoning was that if he thought we were a couple, he'd leave you alone."

She touched his arm. "Thanks for rescuing me, Trev, I appreciate it. But I don't think your ploy will work with him. It might even make things worse by stirring up his hunting blood. I'll bet he enjoys making trouble between, er, friends." She hesitated. "And he knows we never met in person until the other day. So how can we be a couple?"

"How, indeed?" he said so softly she almost didn't catch the words.

She decided to stop deepening the hole she was digging for herself, so she added in a brisk tone, "He's an opportunist. He saw me come out of your room, noticed the way I was dressed, or rather my state of undress, and tried his luck. Oh, I just remembered. He asked me out for dinner and dancing some evening. That can be a backup opportunity for your room search, if I can't get him to ask me to the preview or the sale."

Trev's British accent swiftly became very crisp. "Oh, he did, did he? And how did you respond?"

"I told him at the time that I was tired from traveling and wanted to settle in. I...hinted that we might go out another time."

A sudden frown creased Trev's forehead, and his eyes glittered like sunlight reflecting off the English Channel. "And you'd go out with him? Alone? After this morning?"

She swallowed the zing of fear that shot through her. "For you and for Penwith, I'll *accompany* him. Once, if things work out. Please, let's use this, Trev."

His posture was unnaturally rigid and tension emanated from him as they walked, almost at a march. In a voice to match, he said,

"'Accompanying' him or on a date, you'll still be alone with him."

"I can handle time alone with him, just not long or often." She adopted a calm, reasoning tone for his sake. "I'll simply make sure he's out of your way. If I get any information out of him that might help us figure out what's going on here, I'll consider it a bonus."

Trev wasn't soothed or distracted. "That's a two-way street. He might try to get information out of you. He's already tried, if you'll recall. So, Reynaldos kissed your hand, asked you out, and pinned you to the wall last night? Is that the correct sequence of events?" He broke the eye contact she found so telling.

She felt cautious hope. This obviously went beyond Trev's concern for a friend's safety. His spoken words and body language hinted at deeper feelings, whispering to her just out of hearing. Then there were the two kisses they'd shared.

"There were...several inches of space between us last night." Now she was the one avoiding eye contact. Remembering the feel of Sebastian's lips on her skin, she wiped her hand on her jeans and the tiny smile slipped from her face. "I've told you I don't like it when he touches me. I'm not encouraging him, Trev."

"I'm very glad to hear it," he said in a clipped tone. "Look, Ellie, Reynaldos plays rough. I should send you to London until I have something I can take to the police, or enough time has passed to justify my throwing him out of Penwith. Something other than my great dislike of the man."

He was pulling back, suggesting actions that would separate them. She couldn't let that happen. She confronted him in the street, halfway to Jock's garage.

"Send me? I don't think so, Trev, because I won't be sent." She crossed her arms over her chest. "I will leave Penwith, though, if you want me to." There was a definite wobble to the words.

"I don't think so, Ellie."

A frown shadowed Trev's golden, sun-touched face. They stared at each other while a gentle breeze buffeted them, around them and between them, with the smell of the sea riding its crest.

"You're crazy, too, Ellie." His voice was soft and warm and brimming with laughter now. "You're as crazy as I am. When did yours start?"

She swallowed hard and met his eyes squarely, knowing that neither of them was talking about Sebastian Reynaldos. "Oh, about eighteen years ago, I'd say."

"That sounds just about right for me, too. Be careful, Ellie. Don't forget the man just tried to kill us."

"He tried to kill *you*, Trev. I told him last night that I was walking to Avallen to meet you. I wasn't supposed to be in that Land Rover with you this morning."

His answering words brought her to silence. "Messing about with people's brakes isn't an exact science. Did you notice he didn't allow you any room to change your mind?"

Chapter Seven

JOCK DECLARED THE Land Rover roadworthy when they returned to the garage, despite the vehicle's unusual activities that morning. It had received the full attention and tender ministrations of Jock himself, plus his two part-time helpers. Being a curiosity, Penwith's Land Rover would generate free drinks in The Fair Trader for a week for the tellers of its acrobatic adventures. Jock had even taken pictures before he winched it up the cliff face. The reason for its odd behavior was held among Jock, Trev, and Ellie.

"The Spaniard is out but due any minute," Reilly told them in a tired voice when they arrived at the house. Trev looked at him closely, giving him a light pat on the back as he passed him. A nerve jumped in the older man's weathered cheek.

The Land Rover sat on the forecourt for Sebastian to see upon his return. Trev disappeared upstairs, searching for the two electricians who were to start work in the passage, wiring lights for tours. Ellie shivered when she remembered where they would be working.

Refusing her offer of help, Reilly and Annie assembled the 'cold collation' on the buffet in the dining room. Ellie doubted she'd be interested in it by lunchtime. Gathering her books, she took them to the library to work, glad that Sebastian and his laptop were nowhere to be seen.

An hour later, she flung open the door and barreled through the doorway, without looking, on her way to an urgent rest stop. The effects of their teashop visit lingered. She stifled a little scream when she came up against Sebastian's broad chest.

"*Buenos dias*, Ellie."

His hands moved to her shoulders to steady her. Despite their light touch, she felt as if she was being caressed by a tiger. She fought the powerful urge to pull away then tell him what she thought of him. But she couldn't do that, or reveal that his touch gave her chills. She was voluntary bait who would lure him away from the house so Trev could safely search his room. She could, however, step back.

"Good morning, Sebastian." She injected warmth into the words.

Over his shoulder she saw Trev come part way down the stairs. He stopped when he saw them, his face an unreadable mask. He quietly turned and went back up. She felt a moment of panic. Surely he wouldn't attempt to search Sebastian's room now?

She stepped aside so Sebastian could enter the library. "Reilly's lunch buffet is almost ready. I'll join you for a cup of tea, if you like."

He made a gesture of distaste. "*Gracias*, but I cannot face a cold lunch buffet just yet, and I do not like tea. Will you walk with me in the garden instead?"

After a trip to the downstairs bathroom, she rejoined him. They opened the library's French doors onto the flagstone terrace at the side of the house. From there, broad, shallow steps led to the first level of garden. He pulled her hand into the crook of his elbow.

In this top level of terraced garden, she noticed that some of the borders had been dug out and replanted, probably the work of Reilly and Annie. Other beds were still in their wild state with the remains, according to Reilly, of last year's yellow and Himalayan poppies prominently rampant in the brush among the ancient tulip trees, Chinese rhododendrons, and Japanese magnolias. She would have to take his word for it.

She turned to look at the garden's view of the imposing granite house with its decoration of soft green, red, and bright yellow lichens.

"Do you know the history of Penwith house, Sebastian?" If she bored him stupid every time he got near her, maybe there would be less hand kissing and smoldering looks. "I've been researching Penwith, and Trev told me its history in his letters. I've never forgotten."

He patted her hand and tried to turn her away from the house. "My home in Spain is equally venerable, I assure you."

She pulled back. "Stop that! If you want to herd me and pat my hand, or if you really believe I don't think for myself, then I'll go inside and you can walk alone."

A slow smile played around his sensuous lips. "My apologies, Ellie. I'll be nice."

"Thank you. I'm sure your home is wonderful, too, and I'd like to hear about it. But I'd appreciate it if you'd listen to this because it's what I plan to use in the brochures. More or less."

He nodded briefly. "If it pleases you, I will listen. I will be your 'sounding board.' Yes?"

She eyed him but he didn't laugh at her. "Penwith house began in the fifteenth century as a fortress built on the cliffs above the valley. In the late Tudor era it was pulled down, and a house was built here at the head of the valley. Trev's ancestors used the old stone from the keep and from the curtain walls of the fortress to build it.

"During England's Civil War, the Sinclairs and Penwith stood for Charles the First against Cromwell. Early in the eighteenth century, the heyday of fair-trading, most of the left wing was rebuilt.

"The stones of Penwith, as it stands today, have sheltered the Sinclair family for centuries against the Cornish wind, rain, and sun." Sebastian made impatient little moves. She ignored them. "During the rebuilding that was done, the stones were handled with special care to protect the lichens—"

"Very interesting," he interrupted and turned them to face the sea. "The tourists will be pleased. Do you have plans for this afternoon, Ellie?"

"Only to recover from my brush with death this morning," she said with more heat than she intended. Pulling her arm out of his, she looked up at him. "It's becoming tiresome."

His tanned face turned a shade lighter. "What did you say?"

She glanced at the sea for a moment and forced a calm into her voice, a calm she didn't feel as she relived those frightening moments. "Trev lost the brakes on the Land Rover this morning when we were driving to Avallen." She turned back to him, wanting to see his reaction. "We went over the edge of the cliff road but a ledge stopped us. As you can see, we're all right. Even the Land Rover is all right. We were very lucky." She ended with a definite gulp.

His features tightened but she didn't see any of the emotions she was looking for, like horror, regret, or remorse. "I find Sinclair lax in many ways, but to toy with your safety is unforgivable!"

She stared at her feet instead of shouting nasty things in his face. "It was a faulty brake line and not Trev's fault at all." A change of subject was definitely called for or she would soon fly at him like Traveller in a temper. "Why did you ask if I had plans?"

"I must drive to Penzance this afternoon for a short appointment. Will you come with me? We can do a tour, if that pleases you."

Perfect. She'd haul Trev out of the passage and he could search Sebastian's room today. And her rental, unused since her arrival, still sat on the forecourt.

"Are you familiar with the phrase 'Kill two birds with one stone,' Sebastian?" If he wasn't, he should be. She wondered where she found the nerve to quote it to him. "I have to turn in my rental car in Penzance. If I drive it in, will you pick me up after your appointment? I'd really appreciate it because I'm not using it. We can see Penzance then drive home together."

He pursed his lips. "Very well. At least I will have your company on the return journey."

They made their plans for after lunch then she realized she still had to fulfill her promise to walk with him.

"I don't believe I've ever met a collector of rare antique jewelry before. Is it a big sale in Treborne, lots of antique jewelry?"

"Sixteenth-century jewelry," he corrected. "My passion. A very small part of the sale, I believe." He paused. "May I ask you something, Ellie? And please do not tell Sinclair I have asked. Has he ever mentioned to you a cross? A jeweled cross?"

Gray-blue sky, gray-green water, and one large white cloud with bruised edges blurred together for just a second.

"You are silent, Ellie. There is no reason for *you* to be afraid of me." His tense voice let her know he was watching for her slightest reaction, as she had his a moment ago.

She shouldn't be afraid of him? She was in the Land Rover when it went over a cliff. Had he already forgotten that bit of his handiwork? Her fingers had brushed the flakes of destroyed parchment pages from her jeans, another act of destruction that was down to him.

"A jeweled cross? Not that I recall." She handled it rather well, considering the words squeezed past her heart, which had leapt into her throat when he asked.

His voice changed subtly and his body tensed. "The cross was a...a tale in my family, a tale I now know has a basis in fact. It is a family heirloom that rightfully belongs to me. I have heard that Sinclair has it in his possession."

She attempted a tiny laugh of disbelief, but her suddenly dry mouth turned it into a short hiss. "Who told you Trev has it? He's never mentioned that he—"

"The cross is more of a legend in his family, I believe. The truth is that one of Sinclair's ancestors killed one of my ancestors who survived the Spanish Armada in 1588. She took the cross from his body."

She wavered, wondering if the Sinclair family story was the truth. Trev said the villagers would have killed the Spaniard if they'd found him while the battle raged. What if Elizabeth Sinclair had been a patriot rather than a romantic? Had the cross come into Trev's family in a violent way instead of one brought by love?

But Don Alonso de Reynaldos had lived and returned to Spain to father children there. And when she remembered the cross itself, she was ashamed of her moment of doubt. She recalled its warmth when she touched it and when it rested against her skin. No evil was associated with the Spaniard's cross, only warmth and love. Trev's family story was true, she was sure of it.

"What an interesting story," she finally said. "Did you say she?"

He ignored that question, too. "I want what is mine." And he stopped walking, ruining her plan to accidentally kick him. Just once.

So, she repeated her first question. "Who told you Trev has this cross?"

"Someone who knows of my collection and who also knows the erroneous story held by Sinclair's family. No detail escapes me in my pursuit of something that belongs to me. Or of something I want."

Geoff or Inez? She tugged on his arm to set them walking again. She'd simply have to fight her kicking urge. "You want this cross very badly. Have you discussed this with Trev?"

His face told her he was a man at war with himself. To confide or not to confide? "Sinclair refuses to acknowledge he has the cross. His belief that the cross is his family heirloom is fantasy. They acquired it through thievery and desecration."

"If you have a claim to this cross and you believe Trev has it, then why don't you pursue the matter legally?"

"A great deal depends upon my possessing the cross." The words burst forth in a low, intense rush. He reined in both his words and himself. "This is personal and private, a matter of family pride. Pride is everything to a Spaniard." The pressure of his arm pressing hers against his body verged on pain.

She gasped and tried to pull away. His grip eased and he muttered an apology, but he wouldn't free her.

"You won't do anything silly, Sebastian? A piece of jewelry, even with family ties, isn't worth hurting another human being, family pride or not. Talk to Trev."

Sebastian's mouth was a tight, straight line, and his dark eyes flickered with fire. "Sinclair does not know who he is dealing with. I *will* have the cross, Ellie, at any cost, and I will not talk him out of it."

The disturbing gleam in his eyes and the fierceness of his voice made her pull away from him. Trev's voice saying, "barking mad," came into her head. Had this man who stood before her really tried to kill Trev, after destroying the pages in the parish records? Her answer was a wave of coldness washing over her.

At that moment, she didn't doubt that Sebastian would move on to more desperate measures and more desperate acts to possess the cross. The fragile facade he wore was crumbling. If she had to spend time with him to keep him away from the house, then this conversation had to move in other directions. The alternative was to run screaming to her room, adopt a fetal position, and suck her thumb until Trev removed Sebastian from Penwith.

She summoned up a smile and lied. "I'll keep your confidence, Sebastian, but I can't help you. I'm sorry."

"*Gracias.*" He had regained control of himself, but his emotional high now turned in her direction. He grasped both her hands and brought them to his lips. "You stir my blood, Ellie. I will soon leave England. Come with me. Visit Spain, as my guest."

While Sebastian placed warm, moist, jolting kisses on each of her palms, she glanced up at Penwith. Trev leaned out of a window on an upper level, watching them. His pinched, worried face certainly didn't reflect seething jealousy, but there was hope, as long as he didn't fall out of the window.

She pulled her hands out of Sebastian's grasp. "You're an attractive man, Sebastian, but I'm not looking for a love affair. I came to England and to Penwith to heal. Thank you for inviting me to visit your country. I've always wanted to see Spain, but my time away from my job is limited and I've committed it here."

He smiled, eyes and teeth glinting. "Do not forbid me to touch you, Ellie, because I find I am unable to honor that request."

Her tongue took a sudden vacation from her brain. "Oh. No...I..."

"Good. I will attempt to change your mind, on many points. Will you come out with me tomorrow as well, Ellie? I've been invited to preview the private part of the estate sale near Treborne. The sale is the following day. Pieces of Armada jewelry are being offered, and my sources tell me that several of them are outstanding. I'd like to see them and perhaps bid on them. May I show them to you?"

She was stunned at the ease with which she could be thrust into his company for hours and hours. It would give Trev the time he needed tomorrow, if he didn't search Sebastian's room today.

She couldn't bring herself to accept outright, however. "After taking off this afternoon... How long would we be gone tomorrow?"

Her hint of acceptance brought a coaxing tone to his voice. "We will leave after lunch and you'll be back at Penwith in time for dinner. Come. Help me choose the perfect piece for my collection."

She'd have to accept, for now. But Trev had better make good use of the time she was giving him today.

She unclenched her teeth. "Since you're a knowledgeable collector, how can I resist? I'll probably ask so many questions, you'll be sorry you invited me."

"I doubt that. Since you enjoy the English afternoon tea, we can include that tomorrow. Time to go in, I think. It's beginning to rain," he said as he opened the library's French doors for her. His hand slid down to the small of her back to guide her through.

She hadn't noticed the clouds rolling in. She looked back at curtains of misty rain floating across the gardens where it had been sunny a moment ago.

Trev had educated her on the Cornwall peninsula's reputation for fickle weather, like perpetual spring that varied from mile to mile. While the coasts and the headlands might be socked in with a cold fog, isolated valleys could be clear and enfolded in warm stillness. But, surrounded by the sea, Cornwall was subject to violent storms that lashed and roared, tearing hills, valleys, and coasts alike.

Sebastian, skipping out on Reilly's lunch buffet, left for Penzance, and she agreed to follow as soon as she changed clothes. She went to the kitchen to break the news to Reilly and to ask where Trev was working in the passage and how she might get his attention. Reilly was still making pasties while Annie chopped potatoes and fresh herbs for him. The room was warm and steamy, full of meat and pastry smells.

His skill with the short dough briefly distracted her from her mission. "Are you freezing them? You're making so many."

Annie spoke up. "These have potatoes in them, miss, so we won't freeze them. Penwith's kitchen supplies The Fair Trader with pasties one day a week."

"We'll have enough for us for a few days, never fear," Reilly reassured her. "We reheat them in a low oven. They're a favorite of the guv's." Reilly's respect and fondness for Trev was there, in his words.

Reilly suggested that she call Trev's name into the passage from his bedroom. After he gave her the key to Trev's bedroom door, she took the back stairs two at a time. An unnerving stillness overlaid the half-light of the hall, making her tap on Trev's door before she let herself in.

The panel at the back of his fireplace stood open. Cool moist air flowed out of it into the room. A metal basket full of small logs from the hearth held it open. She glanced at the dark hole, even walked up to it, but when she put out a trembling hand, she drew back with a gasp as a smothering sensation settled over her. Closing her eyes, she called Trev's name into that all-encompassing darkness. She staggered back and watched the blackness lighten until the beam of a flashlight became brighter and brighter.

Trev came out of the passage carrying it. He glanced behind her at the closed door of his room. "I'm glad your little *tête-à-tête* with Reynaldos is over."

"And I'm glad you didn't fall out of the window, but my *tête-à-tête* with Sebastian is just beginning." She told him about her imminent journey to Penzance and to the sale preview the following day. "If you search his room now, I can get out of the trip tomorrow."

He frowned. "Blast! There's a hitch in the plans for the passage lights. I'm going into Treborne with Thomas and the lads to return some supplies and choose new. They're waiting for me now. If you're not here when I get back, I'll have a go at it then."

"No, don't. Please. If you can't start now, then leave it until tomorrow. My nerves won't stand it."

"Be careful, Ellie. I ought to simply chuck him out." A dark look at his bedroom door accompanied the words. "Geoff answered my e-mail. He'll send the results of his search on Reynaldos tomorrow. He'll be here himself the day after but I don't have a time yet."

"You probably should just chuck him out, but I've committed myself to spending two afternoons with him so you can search his room. He says he's going back to Spain shortly, and he asked me about the cross."

When Trev had heard every detail of their conversation, he sighed. "'I don't know who I'm dealing with' and 'a great deal depends on his possessing the cross?' What the hell does all that mean? Beg off today, Ellie. Please."

"I can't! He's already left. I should take back my rental car anyway." Her stomach did a bungee jump to her feet when she saw the look on his face. "Why? What's happened?"

"There's been another rather sad and scary development. Inez Concepcion was killed in a road accident ten days ago. Geoff is very upset."

Her first thought was for Trev's friend. "Oh, poor Geoff." Then she remembered where Inez might fit into the Sebastian equation. "Oh," she added.

"Exactly. The brakes failed on her vintage car. She died instantly from the crash."

Chapter Eight

TREV, HIS FLASHLIGHT, and the black hole behind him spun around her for several seconds before she was able to think clearly again.

"Tell me that Inez's accident might be a coincidence. Remind me that we don't have concrete proof that our brakes had been tampered with, or that Sebastian destroyed the pages in the parish records. Please."

His eyebrows traveled upward into his forehead. "You just did. I'll grant you that so far our suspicions have been based on two things: coincidence and a connect-the-dots theory that matches the facts with the most likely perpetrator. But the coincidences are mounting, and all fingers point toward Sebastian."

She swallowed. Hard. "You're right. I'm just trying to rationalize so I don't have hysterics while I'm with him. I don't think he'll hurt me, unless I annoy him. And trust me, I don't intend to annoy him, today or tomorrow."

He pinned her with a look. "And what if he wants to make mad, passionate love to you? That annoys—er, that would annoy the hell out of me."

She gasped, imagining Trev making any kind of love to her. "I'll think of something. If I'm not back in time for dinner, send out a search party."

She dressed in her best jeans and a nice sweater. Because of the weather, she pulled her rain slicker out of the closet and shrugged it on.

THE CITY OF Penzance sat on the Lands End Peninsula of Cornwall. The drive took longer than Ellie expected, but she enjoyed seeing the countryside. She arrived at the car rental office fifteen minutes before Sebastian pulled up, enough time to conduct her business and not keep him waiting.

Wearing a lightweight overcoat, he kept up a steady patter of conversation while he helped her into his rented sports car. She settled onto the cushioned seat beside the Spaniard, her fingers playing over the seat's smooth, soft leather surface. The car's engine stirred with a purring growl that hinted at reserves of power held tightly in check.

The man driving the car gave the same impression. He handled the car expertly and with ease.

"I have hired a guide for a few hours, if that meets with your approval. She tells me Penzance should be discovered on foot. Many of the areas are for pedestrians only."

"That will be great. Walking is just what I'm supposed to do."

MEGAN, THE GUIDE, was firmly under Sebastian's love spell, sending him smoldering, melting looks when she thought Ellie wasn't looking. Once when Megan turned away after such a look, Ellie sent Sebastian a tiny wink. He drew himself up to his full height, his features wooden. He was more displeased when she grinned.

Megan's commentary was brisk and informative. She took them down Market Jew Street, the main street. They visited two museums, and Ellie window shopped, going down some of the narrow side streets and alleys that dated back to the sacking of the town by the Spaniards in 1595.

In Chapel Street, Sebastian refused to tour the Church of St. Mary the Virgin and opted to smoke outside instead. They ended up at Penzance's bustling, working harbor, filled with local fishing boats, a few yachts, and one traditional sailing ship with towering masts.

On the return journey up Chapel Street, both the librarian and the reader in Ellie were thrilled to see the home of Maria Branwell, who married Reverend Patrick Bronte and became the mother of Charlotte, Emily, Anne, and their brother Branwell.

Since Mount's Bay was on their route home, they followed Megan to Marazion. At the heart of the bay stood St. Michael's Mount, a rocky, wooded island crowned by a former Benedictine Priory and a romantic castle. The tide was in, so the 500-yard-long granite causeway was covered. They opted for a boat trip around the island, which their boatman called a 'rounder.'

Ellie was determined to see it all again, in more detail, with Trev. She yearned to tour the gardens and visit every history-filled room of the Mount with him at her side.

After Ellie thanked Megan, she glimpsed Sebastian giving the tour guide a good-bye kiss that reduced the woman to one quivering hormone. In fact, Ellie suspected that Sebastian arranged the macho display for her benefit. If she didn't want him, other women did and he wanted her to know what she was missing. He reinforced her impression by bringing up the subject when they were alone, heading home to Penwith.

"Megan and I are...acquainted." His displeasure with her teasing had passed, apparently, because a cocky grin accompanied the words.

"I'll bet you are. Why aren't you married, Sebastian, a big, handsome guy like you? Or maybe you are."

"No, I am not. Why please just one woman when I can please many?"

"So many women, so little time?"

"Exactly."

"Are you familiar with the term 'male chauvinist pig,' Sebastian?"

"Intimately. It has been hurled at me several times."

"Then I won't bother hurling it again."

He laughed before sending her a considering look. "You are the only woman I have ever permitted to speak to me in such a way."

"Permitted?" There was a sharp edge on her voice as she wondered what consequences there had been for the others. "No one 'permits' me to speak the truth."

"I find that from you, I like it," he continued, ignoring her temper. "Both the attitude and the words. I have a very pleasant reaction to your sharp tongue. You interest me very much. Do you believe in reincarnation, Ellie?"

She thought of Trev and how she recognized his kiss that first night under Penwith's roof. "I might."

"If I believed in anything, I would believe you and I belonged to each other in another time."

She was struck dumb for a moment, but only for a moment. "If you were mine in another lifetime, Sebastian, I probably strangled you with one of your gold chains. What tempts you to suddenly consider belief in reincarnation?"

"You, Ellie. What I feel when I touch you. You tempt me away from my purpose in coming to England. Don't pretend you don't feel something when my skin touches yours because I have seen it. I have felt it."

Her hands balled into fists on her lap. "Okay, I won't pretend or deny it. I feel something, but whatever it is comes from you into me, not from inside me. It's not totally pleasant, Sebastian." She thought of Trev's kisses and the toe-curling thrills that surged from the depths of her being. There was no comparison.

"There is time. I haven't gone beyond kissing your hands. Yet." He flashed her a look that nearly fogged up the windows.

She didn't dwell on the look or the thought. "You said 'If I believed in anything.' Are you saying that a nice Catholic boy like you doesn't believe in anything spiritual, Sebastian?"

He looked away from the road again for a moment. "Consider the freedom, Ellie. If there is no heaven, no hell, then all things are permissible."

She shivered. "You're scaring me now."

"Good. A woman should never lose the tiny primal fear she has of a man who wants her."

She dwelled silently on those words for the rest of the drive.

Trev, Thomas the electrician, and Thomas's 'lads' were unloading a van when they roared onto the forecourt. Trev looked a question at her and visibly relaxed when she gave the tiniest nod that she was okay. Sebastian excused himself and went straight to his room to prepare for a conference via computer in the library later that night. He asked Trev to send up his dinner on a tray. Trev pulled his forelock in an angry gesture to Sebastian's retreating back.

When the workmen left, the house grew still around them. Reilly had borrowed the Land Rover to drive Annie to a movie. The only thing that disturbed their candlelit dinner of warmed pasties in the kitchen was her report on her afternoon with Sebastian. They adjourned to the library to work on her master plan for Penwith's promotional campaign.

But Ellie couldn't concentrate, distracted by her mental rehashing of Sebastian's every word. She'd managed very well through dinner, but now... What Sebastian said about reincarnation especially preyed on her mind.

"Ellie, what's wrong? I've just repeated something twice and you still didn't hear."

"Sorry, Trev. It was a long day."

"No, I'm sorry. You're not having much of a holiday, are you? The only exciting bit was going over the cliff."

She laughed. "Then please spare me any more exciting bits. And please don't think I'm not enjoying myself, because I'm having a wonderful time. There's nothing I'd rather do right now than get to know you better and help in my small way to present Penwith to the world."

"What you're doing is no small contribution, Ellie." He paused. "I've been told I'm a good listener. Tell me why you're so preoccupied tonight. Did this morning bring back painful memories of your own accident? Or did Reynaldos upset you today in some way you haven't told me?"

"The answer to the first question is yes, briefly, but I'm okay now. As for the second... Upset? No. He said something that disturbs me, though."

He sat up straighter. "He didn't suggest—? He didn't want to—?"

Her cheeks tingled beneath her furious blush, delaying her answer. When Trev spluttered and rose up out of his chair, she laid a hand on his arm.

"No, Trev, nothing like that. It's hard to explain without giving you the wrong impression."

"Ellie, please be kind and put me out of my misery."

"Only if you promise to really listen to what I'm saying. Don't read anything into it."

He took her hand. "I promise I'll try. How's that?"

She didn't want to go into this with Trev, not when she couldn't tell him what she felt when he touched her compared to what she felt when Sebastian touched her.

She took a deep breath. "When Sebastian touches me...I feel something." She squeezed his hand when she saw his face change. "It's something that flows out of him into me, not my reaction to him. He dared me today to deny I felt it. I told him then what I'm telling you now."

"I suppose women think he's handsome. I—"

"Listen to me, Trev. It's not a nice feeling. Not like when you—" She caught herself. "It's like a jolt of electricity, cold electricity, if you can imagine that."

"Then you're not attracted to him?"

"Fascinated by him is more like it. The way a tiger's beauty and grace would fascinate me, despite the danger. He believes I was his in another life." She felt him go tense and still.

"And do you believe that?" he asked quietly.

"No, I don't. I wasn't *his* in another life."

To cover her slip, she repeated what she'd told Sebastian about her strangling him with one of his gold chains. Trev's resulting laugh thrilled her.

"But you do believe in reincarnation?"

She gave him a quick smile. "He asked me that, too. I could be convinced."

He looked away, twirling her pen with the thumb and forefinger of his free hand. "I asked because you feel...familiar, to me. When I kissed you the other night and today..."

Her gaze flew to his face. "Me, too! You didn't say."

"Because it frightened the hell out of me." He sent her a lopsided grin. "And you're certain that what you felt those two times was nothing like you feel with Reynaldos?"

She shivered. "I'm positive."

"I think we need more research, and I'm not about to kiss Reynaldos to compare. Close your eyes, Ellie. Please?"

Instead she opened them wide. "What? Why?"

"I promise I won't hurt you or anything like that. Mine will be closed, too. Turn your chair to face mine, then scoot forward on it and close your eyes."

At first she felt nothing except his knees against hers. Then there was gentle warmth. Body heat. Trev must have leaned forward, closer to her. A tickle on her cheek. Then, a touch on her hair, following its length to where it split in a silky waterfall over her shoulders. The tips of the rounded cushions of his fingers touched her eyelids, slid down the curve of her cheeks to her mouth. The warmth turned to fire, and she remembered that fire. A tear of joy and recognition slipped down her face as his fingertip trailed across the points of her upper lip and swept across the fullness of her lower. Her lips parted and she gasped.

Turnabout was fair play, and she couldn't have stopped herself if she'd tried. Her hands lifted to his face. Touching his cheeks, she leaned toward his warmth, slipping one knee between his to bring them even closer. His hair was thick and sleek to her touch, just as she imagined it would be. The tips of her index fingers followed the curves of his ears then down the sides of his neck to find his pulse beating wildly at its base. Her thumbs outlined his lips from the center of his upper to meet midpoint on his lower. They parted beneath her touch as a sound, part sob, part groan, escaped him. Then her fingers moved back into his hair and she sought his lips with her own. And the familiar fire turned into an inferno.

Ten minutes later, she was aware that Sebastian had walked into the room. By then they were sitting back in their chairs, staring at each other across several feet of space.

Sebastian's voice was taut. "Forgive my intrusion. I—"

"Go away, Reynaldos," Trev interrupted in an exhausted voice, a grin of delighted amazement on his face.

His rudeness shocked her enough that she broke eye contact with him. Sebastian's eyes burned into her.

He held up his laptop case. "If you'll recall, I have a conference in fifteen minutes."

"Oh. Sorry." Trev got to his feet and pulled her to hers. "Come along, Ellie."

Sebastian's eyes were on their clasped hands as they left the room. She couldn't wait for the door to close between them and the man in the library.

Trev paused in the hall. "Would you like a drink in the sitting room?"

"No. Thanks. I'm exhausted. Whatever happened in there...I need to think."

He dropped a kiss on her forehead. "I know, and we have to talk, Ellie, but I can't say what I want to say to you until Reynaldos is out of this house. After I search his room tomorrow, I'll give him notice to vacate, that I need the room or something."

She nodded, still unable to form complete sentences. A minute later she went to bed. Alone.

Chapter Nine

SHE SAW LITTLE of Trev the next morning. The work in the passage had reached critical mass and he was needed there. She walked to Avallen and met with several business owners, outlined a cooperative promotion plan, and received commitments from each of them.

Early in the afternoon, she went down the stairs to meet Sebastian. He waited for her at the front door, appreciation evident in his eyes as he examined her from head to toe.

She wore the only items of clothing she'd brought with her that would do. They were a broomstick skirt that rippled when she walked and a white tee shirt with embroidery, interwoven with pearls, around the neck in colors that matched the rainbow of hues in the skirt.

She'd belted the tee over the skirt then twisted her hair, winding it around her head and holding it with her pearl hair combs. In deference to the changeable weather, she added a long sleeved white linen shirt over her tee. Strappy sandals completed her outfit.

Sebastian wore a tweed sport coat over his dress shirt and slacks. He'd ruined the sedate look by adding a scarlet silk cravat that showed at his neck. The slash of color and the flash of gold on his fingers and wrists made him stand out as a stranger to English shores.

He paused to give her a cool, searching look when he got into the car with her. She returned it, solemn and unblinking. Other than that he gave no indication that seeing her with Trev in the library last night bothered him.

The sporty car rolled smoothly along the country lanes. A morning mist had moved on, leaving the road surface wet in spots. Sebastian drove fast on the narrow roads but with great control. It was as though he, and therefore the car, anticipated every bump and curve.

"Treborne is on the moors, isn't it?" she asked.

"Yes, the Penwarren house is just outside the village." So far, his eyes hadn't left the road. "I have an appointment at four to view the pieces privately and to submit my bids."

"And the items won't be auctioned in the usual way tomorrow?"

"This part of the sale is by invitation only. I might be bidding against museums," he added, pride and anticipation in his voice.

"Is your collection famous, Sebastian?" At least he hadn't lied to

Trev about that.

He shrugged and pouted his lips in a continental gesture. "Only among other private collectors. My collection contains the finest examples of sixteenth-century Spanish jewelry to be found outside museum collections. Some pieces have been in my family for generations, others came from treasure ships that were making their way from Mexico to Spain when they sank in storms. My special pieces are, of course, Armada jewelry."

Having seen the Spaniard's cross, she understood why a serious collector might yearn to own such a lovely piece of craftsmanship. But how many would want to possess it enough to kill for it, sight unseen? Maybe Trev would find something today in Sebastian's room to explain it, or maybe Geoff's information, when he sent it, would shed light on this obsession.

The Menhoth Inn in Treborne offered shepherd's pie as their afternoon special. Sebastian ordered it for both of them, plus he consumed several pints of the inn's best bitter. The look in his eyes had ratcheted up several degrees by the time he was well into his second pint.

He reached for her left hand, examining the gold and amethyst ring Trev had sent her after the accident. "Tell me again how you met Sinclair?"

"Trev and I wrote to each other when we were children. Pen pals. We just didn't stop when we grew up. When he took a leave of absence from his job to renovate the house, he offered Penwith to me as a healing place. A sanctuary."

"Sanctuary?" He looked up at her.

A wave of dark hair had fallen forward onto his brow. He was classically beautiful, in a dark way. She paused, overwhelmed by the impression that this man was the reverse image of Trev, the photographic negative. Sebastian was dark and dangerous compared with Trev's light and love.

"Yes, sanctuary. I mentioned to you I'd been involved in a car a-accident. It took a long time to get well again, including hospitals and physical therapy that went on forever." She filled in a few more sketchy details for him.

"But he did not offer himself as your...sanctuary?" He watched her closely.

"No, not himself." She looked away.

"And you never met him until you came to England a few days ago?" Amazement was thick in his voice. When she confirmed it, he added, "Then Trevor Sinclair is a bigger fool than I imagined him to be."

"Trev is no fool, and neither am I." She caught his little smile and tamped down her anger. He wanted to push her, wanted her be indiscreet in the heat of anger. Instinct told her not to expose her soft spots to this man.

"So, what is Sinclair to you? The truth, please." He eyed her closely.

She put down her teacup and met his gaze. "My dearest friend on earth, and I would despise anyone who hurt him."

"Was it friendship going on between you and Sinclair in the library last night?"

He stopped. She waited. Let him wonder if she was going to answer him.

He continued against her wall of silence. "I ask because the last time I saw that look on a man and woman's faces was in a mirror. We were naked and had just made love."

"I owe you no explanation about last night or any other night of my life, Sebastian, but I'll tell you what went on in the library last night. Trev and I discussed reincarnation, because you mentioned it yesterday and it was on my mind. What you saw was the aftermath of an experiment in touch. Familiarity of touch. That's all."

His eyes narrowed. "I see. So Sinclair thinks that you were his in another life? Like me? It seems he and I are at odds over every aspect of things that touch each of us and things that each of us want."

There was renewed interest in his eyes. It made her uneasy, as if he had accepted a challenge she wasn't aware she'd offered. His next words reinforced that feeling.

"Understand me, Ellie. I do not play children's games in libraries with beautiful women. I am more of a man than Trevor Sinclair will ever be. You only have to say yes and I will prove it to you. I am easy to please as long as I get my own way." This time, when he lifted her hand to his lips, she felt the tip of his tongue tickle her palm.

She gasped, jerked her hand back, brought her left wrist to eye level, shot back the cuff of her shirt, and said, "Goodness, look at the time. Twenty minutes to four. We'd better hurry."

He grinned, standing up to help her with her chair. "This visit to Sinclair is more than curiosity and friendship and...sanctuary, on your part, I think."

On her part? After last night's experiment, she still wasn't sure what Trev felt for her, so Sebastian might just have summed up the situation in those three words.

She injected a lighthearted tone into her voice to cover her discomfort. "I'm in England on a journey of discovery. I've discovered Cornwall and you, Sebastian. And you're about to help me discover the world of collecting sixteenth-century Spanish Armada jewelry. Unless we're late." With that, she linked her arm through his and looked up at him with a smile on her face.

"Don't fight the inevitable, *querida*," he said softly and led her to the car.

PENWARREN HOUSE, a gaunt, plain stone building, contrasted with the green and tan of the moor. Its tall chimneys stood out against the gray sky. Cars of every size and color were parked at the side of the road, along the gravel lane leading to the house, and in the forecourt. Tomorrow, during the sale, the vehicles would spill over into the surrounding fields. Today, small groups of people milled around outside, while inside more people moved from room to room while consulting sale catalogues.

Sebastian showed a gilt-edged invitation to the beefy, plainclothes guard at the foot of the stairs in the main hall. The man looked them over impersonally and impartially before he took it from Sebastian's fingers. They were directed up the wide, straight staircase to the floor above. Two men in three-piece suits stood on each side of a door on which hung a plaque with the name of a distinguished London auction house printed in gold letters.

Ellie handed her tiny shoulder bag to one of the men who dumped it and pawed through its contents, while Sebastian submitted to a frisking by the other. Only then were they permitted to enter the room. By then she was grateful for the warm, steady pressure of Sebastian's arm.

When they stepped inside, however, she forgot her nerves and the men outside. The shimmer of gold from within a long line of individually lighted glass display cases stole her breath.

She managed to tear her gaze away when Sebastian introduced her to a man whose Spanish name she didn't hear clearly. She smiled down into the man's small, close-set dark eyes before he darted ahead of them toward the first case. With his quick gestures and high-pitched voice rapidly speaking Spanish, he reminded Ellie of a mouse. A Spanish mouse. His narrative was directed at her. She looked to Sebastian with a question in her eyes.

"He's telling you the history of the pieces," Sebastian explained.

"Many are from shipwrecks of the 'Invincible Armada,' found off the coast of Northern Ireland."

Ellie was shocked into speech. "Northern Ireland? How did Armada ships get up there?"

"The wind changed many times during the days of the sea battle, which moved back and forth in the English Channel. The Spanish ships were eventually blown north."

Remembering Trev's warm, evocative voice when he told her about the Spanish Armada and Elizabeth Sinclair and her Spaniard, Ellie was stunned that Sebastian told this tale of disaster and death with such a lack of emotion. Yet he continued in the same colorless voice.

"They made a run for Spain by way of Scotland and Ireland. The early autumn gales sank some and blew others onto beaches and cliffs. Many of their treasures have yet to be recovered." He took her elbow and urged her forward.

While the little man pranced with impatience, they made their way to the first case. It was lined with gold coins of uneven shapes and unequal sizes.

Sebastian interpreted for her. "These coins were 'struck' in Mexico by Indian slaves who literally struck a piece of gold with a mallet and a seal to form the rough coins."

He dismissed them with a wave of his hand. They lingered over several of the remaining cases, however. In the next was a gold ornament set with two pearls and an emerald.

Ellie studied it for a moment. "What is it?"

Sebastian shrugged. "Perhaps a hat medallion or part of a necklace. The many young aristocrats in the Armada's ranks would have been wearing their finest when they went down with their ships."

Her heart skipped a beat as Don Alonso de Reynaldos stepped into her mind, or rather her mental picture of him did so. He was darkly handsome with brown eyes, much like Sebastian's, although he wasn't tall like Sebastian. Trev had described him as a boy. Maybe he hadn't reached his adult height when he sailed with the Armada. Somehow she knew he liked to laugh. She imagined a devilish sparkle in those brown eyes. She was glad he and his cross had been spared a chill, watery resting place.

As for the other cases, one held a lithe golden jaguar with ruby eyes, the one beside it a ring of lapis lazuli in a setting of gold, another a golden lizard with an upturned tail, and yet another an exotic bird ornament grooming tool. According to a card and drawing inside the case, the bird concealed a foldout toothpick, its tail formed a fingernail cleaner, and the beak and body were a whistle.

While Sebastian engaged in deep conversation with their guide about the bird, Ellie went ahead to a case that held a thin, rather plain gold pendant, roughly heart shaped. Crudely carved into its surface were two hands, the fingers entwined with each other. With the aid of a magnifying glass built into the top of the case, she made out the Spanish words also primitively carved into the heart.

She sensed Sebastian beside her before he read the words aloud. *"No tengo mas que darte."*

"What does it mean?" she asked around the lump in her throat. Already, without knowing what the words meant, she sensed their poignancy and sadness.

"It says, 'I have no more to give thee,'" he replied softly.

Tears filled her eyes as she imagined the Spanish girl who gave the pendant to her young lover before he set sail in glory with the Armada, only to meet his death in the cold waters off Northern Ireland. The lovers' message had a parallel in the story of the Spaniard's cross. In 1588 England, Don Alonso de Reynaldos had nothing but his heart and his family cross to pledge his love to Elizabeth Sinclair.

"Do you like it, Ellie?" Sebastian asked in a strangely gentle tone of voice she'd never from him before. At her tearful smile and nod, he said one phrase in Spanish to the mousy little man at his side. The man's eyes widened, and he jotted something down in his notebook.

Sebastian continued in the same, new voice. "It is yours. A gift."

When she protested, he put one finger against her lips. "No matter what happens to us or between us, it is yours."

Ellie felt a chill at his words. On one hand, Sebastian wouldn't hesitate to hurt Trev, whom she loved, to gain possession of the Spaniard's cross. And on the other, she knew he gave her this gift from the past as a remembrance of something in her that touched him, something that could not quite rise above what might come. She nodded her acceptance of his gift—and his terms.

She thanked him, dried her eyes, and moved on to the next case. In it were rows of round gold buttons the size of large peas. Engraved flowers on their surfaces reminded her of other flowers she'd recently seen engraved on gold.

Before caution could stop her, words of delightful discovery tumbled out of her mouth. "Oh, look! Those are just like the flowers on the chain of the Sp—"

She swallowed the rest of the words and her voice died when she looked up into the dark, icy depths of Sebastian's eyes.

Chapter Ten

"WHY DO YOU not continue, Ellie?" Sebastian's voice was deadly quiet as he wrapped his big fingers around her wrist. "Let me finish the thought for you. The flowers are the same as those on the chain of the Spaniard's cross?"

The fine hairs on her neck stood on end, but she steadied her voice before she spoke. "You're too confident, Sebastian. What makes you think you can finish my thoughts, let alone my sentences for me? What if the flowers remind me of the Spanish lilies that grow wild in the garden at Penwith, in the bed with the chain link border? Or—"

"Do not toy with me," he whispered harshly and pulled her closer to him. "Please. I am not called *El Halcon* without reason. Sinclair has the cross, there in his house, and you have seen it. Is this not so?"

His heavy cologne, combined with the heated recklessness in his eyes, made her stomach twist and turn. Then hot, sudden anger flowed through her, consuming her. The look in his eyes changed to something naked and hot as he watched the change come over her. That added to her anger.

"I'm sick of this, Sebastian," she hissed. "I don't care if there are flowers on the cross, on its chain, or tattooed on your fine ass."

He let go of her as if she were a stinging bee.

She loosed the angry flow of words, heaping them upon his head. "No more questions about Trev or Penwith or a cross. This is between you and Trev. He'll have to answer your questions, because I can't and I won't. Now," she said in a calmer tone after pulling in a breath, "are you going to be nice or do I have to find my own way back to Penwith?"

Suspicion, laughter, and desire fought it out in his eyes. "I have never seen the cross. Sinclair wouldn't show it to me, but he would show it to you."

When she crossed her arms over her chest and silently glared at him, suspicion dropped out. Laughter and desire now shared the brown depths.

"And I can say with confidence that there are no flowers tattooed on my 'fine ass.' It is, however, available for your inspection anytime you choose."

Her anger deflated, leaving her hollow and numb. She smiled in spite of herself. "I'll pass. What am I going to do with you, Sebastian?" She was amazingly close to tears. "No heaven, no hell. It's all up for grabs, isn't it?"

The mousy man peeked at her from around Sebastian's bulk, first on one side then the other. "Um. I think this gentleman would like you to get back to business. Maybe there are other appointments scheduled?"

She felt like a soft serve on a hot day when Sebastian turned his fierce attention away from her. This outing was over, and for her peace of mind, there would be no more. She fervently hoped that all she'd done today paid off in Trev's search.

Sebastian reverted to his charming self on the drive back to Penwith. While he concentrated on the road, Ellie watched him out of the corner of her eye. The man was an emotional chameleon.

"You handle this car as though it were an extension of your body," she said into a lull in their conversation.

"Ah, this car is like..." He hesitated, searching for a suitably scathing comparison. He found it in a field where shire horses pulled a plow. "Like one of those. I like powerful engines, engines that remind me of thoroughbred horses. I have several such engines in the cars I race in Spain."

A racecar driver would know how to drain then puncture a brake line on an old vehicle so the resulting crash would appear accidental.

She swallowed at the thought. "Sounds dangerous, but you enjoy danger, don't you, Sebastian?"

He smiled and his eyes briefly met hers across the width of the seat. "Flirting with death makes me feel alive. I crave the feeling of power, the control I have when my fate rests with me. Whether in the boardroom or on the racetrack, danger is the only thing that makes me aware I am alive. I do not plan to die in my bed."

Her mind went back to her accident and the silence before the screams started. "I thought I was going to die violently and alone. No slipping away while unconscious or in a nice coma. It was the loneliest moment of my life. I pray that I die when I'm positively ancient and in my own bed, surrounded by those I love and who love me."

He shrugged. "Let us hope we both get our wishes."

She nodded and was silent.

A little while later, he smoothly swung the car into Penwith's forecourt. "Are you certain you wouldn't like an evening out?"

She shook her head. "But thank you for a lovely afternoon and for the things you taught me. I've been away two afternoons in a row, so I have to be rested and on my toes tomorrow. The work will pick up even more now, and I don't know where I'll be needed. Trev's old friend is arriving to work in the gardens."

Sebastian turned toward his door. She froze, glad he wasn't looking at her. If Sebastian knew Inez Concepcion, did he also know Geoff? Thank heaven she hadn't said Geoff's name aloud.

She noticed, however, that Sebastian went very still for a moment in the act of opening his door. By the time he reached her side of the car, however, he wore the look of a downhearted little boy who had been denied a treat.

On a sigh, he said, "Then I must go out alone again."

"You're a real Spanish party animal, aren't you? I appreciate these boosts to my ego, Sebastian, but don't kid an old librarian. A man with your looks and charm need never be alone. You know it as well as I do. And don't forget I've met the lovely Megan."

A warm light shone in his dark eyes. "Ah, but too many women have no spirit. I like a woman who pits herself against me." He paused. "Or, a woman I must take from another man."

So she had been right. If he thought Trev had feelings for her, it would make her more attractive to him.

She whistled softly. "You *don't* play nice, do you? Now I understand why you're not married. No woman has pitted herself against you enough to tempt you to the altar."

"Not all men are fools, Ellie. Some are bachelors." He grinned insolently. "However, I must marry soon. I need a son and heir to carry on the Reynaldos name."

No way would she touch that line. She shook her head in mock despair, moving toward the front door before he gallantly offered her the position. "You're living up to everything I've heard about Spanish men."

He smiled and shrugged eloquently, following her. "The pendant will be delivered to you here in the next day or so. I gave an open-ended bid for it, so it is yours." She heard childlike pleasure in his voice.

She paused on the doorstep and turned to him. "Thank you again, Sebastian. And you're sure you want me to have the pendant, instead of adding it to your collection or donating it to a museum? It's a piece of your country's history."

He stepped closer. Her next step back brought her up against the door. With one hand behind her, she scrabbled to get a grip on the ornate latch digging into her spine.

"The pendant's quality is below that of the other pieces in my collection."

Before she realized what he was doing, his hands were in her hair, releasing it from the combs that held it up off her face and neck.

"What a glorious mane of hair you have, Ellie, shining and moving like it lives," he said breathlessly. "It makes a man want to bury his fingers and face in it. It makes him imagine how it would look unbound over your naked shoulders and breasts."

Her eyes widened and her mouth formed a silent "Oh!" Mentally, she crossed her arms protectively over her chest, her hands on her 'naked' shoulders.

She tried to turn in the tiny space he allotted her. Unfortunately, he was too close and the glorious mane in question now tumbled around her face and shoulders and in front of her eyes. Before she could brush it aside, Sebastian twisted his fingers in it and pulled her face to his, whispering something in Spanish. She made a little sound as his lips closed over hers in a kiss that held equal parts of punishment and passion, pain and pleasure. Compared to last night with Trev in the library... He released her and bowed over her hands.

He looked up at her through his dark lashes. His tanned features wore a self-satisfied expression that she longed to slap off his face. "I bought the pendant because it appealed to you. '*No tengo mas que darte.*' And I bid on the bird because it appealed to me. Have a good evening, Ellie." He stepped back and handed her the combs.

She spun around, fighting the ancient door latch, which abruptly gave way beneath her assault. The door swung open into the hall, taking her with it. She landed in Trev's arms.

"Ellie! I thought I heard voices. Hello, Reynaldos," he added coolly.

He took her by the elbow and propelled her toward the stairs. "I want to show you something. We got a lot done today!" He continued in that vein while he marched her up the stairs.

She was keenly aware of Sebastian's gaze following their every step. When they finally moved out of his line of vision, a violent shiver rippled over her.

Inside her room, she locked the door behind them then spun around to face him. "That went well!" She wiped her mouth with the back of her hand, expecting to see red.

"Bloody hell!" Trev declared. His eyes were on her hair then her lips.

She tilted her head back, smoothed her hair with her fingers, and pushed in the combs.

"You've been kissing Reynaldos! You really needn't throw yourself so completely into this, you know." His words dripped sarcasm.

She wondered briefly just how far up his nose she could shove one of her pearl combs. "I have not been kissing Sebastian," she said with as much dignity as she could muster. "Sebastian has been kissing me, without my consent, my encouragement, or my cooperation."

Trev tried to push past her, purpose in every movement. "I'll just have a word—"

"No!" Ellie flung herself spread-eagled across the door. "It was just a kiss on the doorstep, Trev. One kiss. Not a pleasant one, either. Not like—"

He took her chin in his hands, turning her face this way and that. "He's bruised your lips," he whispered. "I'm so sorry, Ellie."

Gently, lightly, and for one second only, his mouth touched her sensitive lips. A white-hot flame leaped through her, head to toe. She was sure she heard it sizzle and snap.

Her feeling of pleasure was rapidly overshadowed by one of shyness. They stood looking at each other in the gray light from the windows. How could she love him like this when she didn't even know him properly yet, and didn't know what he felt for her, other than a physical attraction?

She watched his dear face take on a watchful expression. "That's all? A kiss?"

She smiled and massaged her wrist where Sebastian's fingers had left their mark. "All? Let me see," she said brightly. "Yesterday he invited me to spend the rest of my vacation in Spain with him. Today he didn't try to make mad, passionate love to me, but he bought me an expensive, sixteenth-century, gold, heart-shaped pendant engraved with love words. That kind of thing?"

"That very kind of thing," he fumed. "Why are you rubbing your wrist?"

She tried to hold it against her side, thought better of it, and held it out for him to inspect. "I made a tiny slip about the flowers on the cross's chain. He responded immediately and with enthusiasm. I made up a story, then I got angry and refused to answer any questions about anything. I dumped the whole matter into your lap and threatened to find my own way home."

He closed his eyes and said in a voice that shook, "Will you please tell me everything that happened today so I don't go down there and thrash him instead of throwing him out."

She put the fingers of one hand against his lips and kept them there while she gave him a summary of her afternoon with Sebastian. After assuring him that he now knew everything that mattered, she took her hand away.

The corners of his mouth pulled up into his formidable grin. "The poor devil probably can't help himself. It's that smile of yours, Ellie. I go weak at the knees when I see it. How can that be?"

She smiled the smile and watched a bewildered look appear on his face. "I don't know, but we really should check into it later. Now, please tell me all this was worthwhile."

He blinked and shook himself. She saw by the expression that settled on his face that he had found a revelation in Sebastian's room. He took a sheaf of papers from under his sweater and, with one look at her piled-high table by the windows, spread them out on the bed. She knelt beside him on the floor, his fellow childhood conspirator.

"Here's proof, Ellie, that my family's story about the Spaniard, is true. Reynaldos has an original document written in Don Alonso de Reynaldos' hand, signed by him, and stamped in wax with his seal. Not a photocopy, mind you, but the real document. He must have nicked it from a museum's archives or something. There were several translations with it. I photocopied the whole mess. Here's the English translation."

With their heads almost touching, they used the bed as a desk, leaning on their elbows over the papers. Trev read the words in a hushed voice that trembled.

"*I, Don Alonso de Reynaldos, declare that the one who possesses the Cross of the Reynaldos family also possesses the Reynaldos lands and fortune, should she choose to claim them.*

"*The Cross was given by me on the Fifteenth Day of October, in the Year of Our Lord Fifteen Hundred and Eight-Eight, to one who was bound to me, before God, in heart, body, and soul.*

"*My descendants shall honor this document bearing my seal.*

"*Signed, Don Alonso de Reynaldos, The First Day of January, in the Year of Our Lord, Fifteen Hundred and Eighty-Nine.*"

Trev tapped the paper with his finger. "Where it says, 'should *she* choose to claim them,' he's surely referring to Elizabeth Sinclair, without actually naming her. It was only a gesture on his part, of course. He was back under his family's influence by then and knew he'd never see her again. And here, where it says 'one who was bound to me, before God,' and the date, probably means they were married October 15, 1588, before he returned to Spain, just as we thought."

Ellie pursed her lips in a low whistle. "If we can find the records in Treborne... No wonder Sebastian tried to destroy the church records. According to this, whoever owns the cross owns everything. The young Don was a bigamist, and the Spanish branch of the family isn't the legal heir to anything."

She stopped, sidetracked by something that puzzled her. "Trev, why didn't Elizabeth take the Reynaldos name and let it be known she was a married woman rather than bear the stigma of being an unwed mother? It was her legal right."

Trev's voice held a grim note. "I doubt that all the formal details were taken care of, banns read and so forth. Maybe the Sinclair brother-vicar was simply trying to make an honest woman of his sister in the eyes of God, not man. Plus, the English and the Spanish were bitter enemies when they married.

"But Elizabeth Sinclair passed on the Reynaldos name in a subtle way. We all have. All the Sinclair first sons have the first or middle name Reginald. Reginald is the English translation of the Spanish name Reynaldos."

Ellie crowed with delighted laughter at the beauty of it. "Good for her! And good for her brother, the kindhearted vicar who married them and risked his soul. And good for the fisherman brother who risked his life to take her Spaniard back to his homeland. May they all rest in peace." She looked up to find Trev watching her.

"I've always liked the way you think, Eleanor *Elizabeth* Jaymes," he whispered as he slowly closed the gap between them.

She closed her eyes and summoned enough breath to say, "Same here, Trevor *Reginald* Sinclair."

He paused. "Your poor lips. Let me kiss them and make them better."

"They could use some tender loving care right now."

His lips detoured first to touch her eyelids and the tip of her nose before settling with butterfly softness upon her mouth. Ellie echoed his gentle movements across her lips and leaned into him. For those few moments there was no cross and no Spaniard, then or now. There was only Trev, in her mind and in her heart.

He pulled back and sighed, taking her hands in his. "This hand kissing Sebastian does, is it like this?" With that he dropped a slow, warm kiss on the back of each hand.

Still under the influence of his kiss, she smiled her pleasure.

"Ummm."

"Or maybe like this?" He turned her hands over and pressed a lingering kiss on each palm.

She gasped as heat flooded through her. "It doesn't feel like this when Sebastian does it, Trev."

"Or possibly like this?"

Her right arm rested on the bed. Beginning with a devastating kiss on her inner wrist, his lips followed her inner arm's length to the soft place inside her elbow. She felt the tip of his tongue there, warm and wet against her skin.

She collapsed back on her heels, her breath coming fast and shallow. "N-No, he never did that."

"Good. Just checking. That will be my party piece." Then he kissed her on the mouth again, long and hard.

Trev had any number of party pieces, as far as she was concerned. When she recovered enough to speak, she asked, "What are we going to do about Sebastian, Trev?"

"I'm asking him to leave tonight. I've made arrangements for him to stay at The Fair Trader, if he chooses to accept my efforts on his behalf.

"I'll gather together our suppositions and the dab of circumstantial evidence we have and take the whole lot to the police. I can tell them my suspicions about our accident, backed up by Jock. I can present the cigarette box, the copy of the old Spaniard's document, and copies of any documents I find in Treborne.

"When Geoff gets here tomorrow, I'll break all this to him and hope he'll give a statement. Maybe our police will prod the Spanish police to look more closely into Inez Concepcion's auto accident, especially in view of Reynaldos' experience with race cars."

She folded up the papers, not looking at him. "When will you leave for Treborne and may I come with you?"

He stroked a finger along her cheek. "I'll go on the last train tonight. And I'm asking you to stay here with Reilly and keep an eye on things. I'd hate to give Reynaldos a free shot at Penwith with nobody in charge but Reilly. He's been acting so strangely since Reynaldos arrived that I don't want to leave him here alone. I'll leave the Land Rover, so Reynaldos will think I'm about somewhere.

"We'll tell Reilly everything before I leave and ask him to stay close and on guard for the next twenty-four hours. He's a good man to have at your back in a fight, as Geoff and I learned."

"Trouble on one of the oil platforms?" she asked, spurred by the look of pain on Trev's face.

"No, not on the oil platforms. It's something I want—no, I need—to talk to you about. When the—"

"—time is right. I know." She heard the edge in her voice. "When will that time be, Trev?"

"Soon, Ellie, I promise. I just hope you still have a good opinion of me after I've told you about it. Now, please excuse me while I throw out our first paying guest. Without a refund."

Chapter Eleven

SHE STAYED IN her room after he left her, avoiding the library where she knew Trev would take Sebastian for their little talk. She felt the need to remove all traces of Sebastian's touch, so she showered then dressed in casual clothes. She and Trev would eat with Reilly in the kitchen that evening.

While she waited, she did rough drafts of several brochures on her laptop to show Trev. She realized she had too much material for brochures alone. Only after hearing Sebastian's sports car rev up and drive away did she venture out of her room.

An envelope lay on the carpet outside her door. It was a note from Sebastian. In his bold, almost calligraphic handwriting he said simply, '*I must see you again. I will telephone you.*'

She found Trev standing in the downstairs hall, staring at the closed front door. She put a hand on his arm. "How did it go?"

"He took it badly, like a child being sent away from the party. He demanded I give him the cross, not sell, mind you, but give. He said it again, by the way. 'You don't know who you're dealing with.'"

A wisp of memory floated up, just below the surface of her mind, something Sebastian had said. It would come to her eventually. "Never mind. He's out of the house, at least."

Reilly had made them a lovely roasted chicken dinner. He protested about sitting down with them for a meal and intruding on their privacy, but Trev overcame his objections without embarrassing him. Ellie had a sneaking suspicion Reilly was missing Annie who had gone unexpectedly that afternoon to London to do for a niece with a new baby.

"Such goings on," he declared when Ellie and Trev had related an abbreviated version of their discoveries.

"Reilly," Trev said gently, "won't you tell me what's bothering you?"

The older man looked away, ignoring Trev's change of subject. "So, Miss Elizabeth Sinclair was married to this Spaniard who was shipwrecked on these shores? Does this mean that you, guv, can take away all this Reynaldos fellow owns?"

Trev's look of concern changed to one of surprise. "No. Even if I could press a claim, I wouldn't want to. I'm entitled only to what my parents left me, what I earn with my own hands, and what I can make Penwith bring in."

How could her feelings for this man ever change, she wondered? What could he possibly have done to make him fear her good opinion of him would change when he told her about it?

"Sebastian must believe you'll claim the Reynaldos lands and fortune," she observed, finishing the last bite of creamy mashed potatoes and savory gravy.

"I don't care what Reynaldos thinks. It's *how* he thinks that bothers me. He's demonstrated that he'll ride roughshod over anyone who stands in his way." Trev's eyes rested briefly on her bruised wrist before he finished the last spoonfuls of his thick apple tart served with clotted cream.

A wave of light hair hung over his forehead, the positive image of Sebastian's earlier in the day. She longed to let her fingers smooth his satiny skin, then take a slow journey through his hair. Last night's sample wasn't nearly enough. The corners of Trev's mouth drew up into his planed, tanned cheeks in a little smile when he caught her watching him. That smile warmed her through and through.

Reilly nervously wiped his mouth with the back of his hand. "Guv," he began slowly, "Maybe I should tell you what I saw—"

A piercing meow interrupted him.

The sound jerked Ellie out of her fantasy. "Traveller?" She glanced around the kitchen.

Reilly, who appeared relieved yet a bit frightened, answered. "In the pantry, miss. Having her kittens, I shouldn't wonder. She's made herself a nest in there."

Ellie rose and rushed to the pantry door. It stood ajar a few inches, and she opened it wider. Three tiny kittens, each a different color or combination, cuddled against the curve of Traveller's stomach, making tiny mewing noises. Traveller, sitting up halfway, licked at the fourth kitten, tar black like her own coat. It wasn't moving or making sounds.

Ellie was vaguely aware of saying Trev's name. Instantly he was there, in the doorway, when she grabbed a clean terrycloth dishtowel off a shelf and fell to her knees in front of Traveller.

"Trouble?" Trev asked while Reilly peeked around his arm.

Traveller looked up at her and Ellie swore she saw a mother's plea there. "Oh, no. Not again." She fought for control. "I'll try to help your kitten, if you'll let me," she whispered.

In answer, Traveller laid down, exhausted, to nurse her healthy kittens. Searching the corners of her mind for every tidbit she'd gleaned from the veterinary shows she watched on television, Ellie scooped up the tiny, limp body and vigorously rubbed it with the towel. When that didn't work she started massaging its chest with her index finger.

Her cheeks were wet with tears as she echoed the words of the mother in the crushed car behind hers in the pileup on a foggy highway. "Breathe! Oh, please, baby, breathe!"

Supporting the tiny head, neck, and back, she held the damp, limp kitten upside down and, using a quick downward movement, tried to clear and stimulate the tiny lungs by centrifugal force.

Trev touched her arm. "Ellie, I think you should stop. It's too late. You're upset—"

"No!" The word's savagery surprised her. "I won't let it die! Another baby is not going to die because I can't help it." She sobbed and fought to make herself understood. "A meat baster. Reilly, quickly!"

Trev knelt beside her and a plastic meat baster appeared between them, held by a gnarled hand. She took it and placed the kitten, wrapped in the folds of the towel, between them on the floor.

"Trev, keep massaging its chest while I suction its nose and mouth."

The tip of the baster was too large to fit into the tiny mouth. That was probably a good thing, since she had little control over the force of the suction. She compressed the bulb, made a tiny 'o' with her thumb and forefinger around the kitten's mouth and nose, and inserted the tip into the opening. She slowly released the pressure on the bulb. The baster made a sucking sound. The last thing she could think of to do was put her own lips over her circled fingers and blow gently. The kitten wriggled then made a tentative noise.

When she heard her kitten's squeaking, Traveller rose again on her front feet. Exhausted, Ellie sat back on her heels and let Trev place the kitten where Traveller could continue stimulating it with vigorous licking.

"You did it, Ellie. He's alive."

Trev smiled at her and she couldn't bear it. She flung herself into his arms and gave herself up to reaction.

Trev gathered her up in his arms and staggered to his feet. "Brandy, Reilly. Now, please." He sat down with her in one of the heavy rocking chairs beside the fireplace.

Reilly brought the decanter from the sitting room and a water glass from the sideboard, but he wouldn't pour the stuff himself. He started to clear their dinner things from the table.

Trev splashed some into the glass then into her mouth when she quieted enough that she wouldn't choke. After that, he held her and rocked her until she was ready to talk.

"You must think I'm crazy." She hiccoughed on the words.

"No." He cupped his hand over the crown of her head in a blessing. "There was a lot more going on in there besides a kitten that wouldn't breathe. The accident?" When she nodded, he added, "Why don't you tell me about it now? It might help."

She took a shaky breath. "I came thousands of miles to tell you about it. It was a chain reaction pileup in a heavy fog. Everyone was creeping along, but with one car crashing into another... A tractor-trailer, a lorry, was in front of me. My car was pushed under it.

"A woman was trapped in the car behind me. She was in labor and driving herself to the hospital when she got caught up in the accident. Like me. Like all of us.

"She had the baby, trapped there in that mess of metal and blood. It wouldn't breathe. I lay there, my thigh crushed, sure I was going to bleed to death, listening to her pray and beg her baby to breathe. I started to talk to her, suggesting things to try. I didn't know where she was, where the baby was, whether she could even touch it. Nothing worked. I begged with her. I prayed with her. Then finally I mourned with her.

"After that, Chance came. He was the tractor-trailer's driver. He was injured, too, but he managed to get himself out of the overturned tractor cab. He tried to help us. He couldn't reach the woman or the baby, but he could get one hand to me. He held my hand like he would never let it go. And he had a flashlight against that horrible darkness." Her body relaxed against him as she drew a deep, shuddering breath.

Trev rocked a little faster. "Oh, Ellie, my darling. Why couldn't you tell me before now?"

'Darling' coming from his lips gave her more comfort than anything he'd done so far. "I had to work through it myself until the time was right. But I knew my healing wouldn't be complete until I came here and told you."

"You're safe now. With me."

Weak laughter worked its way up through her. "An obsessive, oversexed, possibly homicidal Spaniard doesn't count?"

"I'd forgotten him for a moment."

She heard the smile in his voice rather than saw it. "What time is your train?"

"Soon." He glanced at his watch. "Will you come to my room with me for a moment first?"

She tilted her head back and looked up at him. "Etchings?" she asked hopefully.

"Another time," he whispered and his grin held warm promise. "I want to check my e-mail before I leave. Geoff. Want to come along?"

They hoisted themselves out of the chair then climbed the back stairs hand-in-hand.

"Let's hope that bright and early tomorrow morning I'll find, somewhere on the pages for October 14, 15, and 16, 1588, in St. Matthew's parish records the entry for a marriage ceremony performed for Elizabeth Sinclair, spinster of this parish, and Don Alonso de Reynaldos, foreigner."

"And that the missing pages from sometime in July and August of 1589 show that a son was born to Elizabeth Sinclair Reynaldos and was baptized," Ellie finished for him.

Penwith's only computer was in Trev's room. He planned to set one up in the library for guests' use, but this one was strictly personal. While he did the necessary things, Ellie walked around his room again, adding to her first impressions of it, of him, from its ambience.

"Jay-sus!" Trev, using one of Reilly's favorite expressions, exclaimed across the room.

"What? What is it?" She hurried to his side.

"Geoff sent this before he left for England today. He came through for us, in spades. As I suspected, and he finally admits, he didn't stop with the old Spaniard. As a surprise for me, he traced the family tree right up to Sebastian Reynaldos' branch and twig. Reynaldos is the last of the Spanish line."

"Sebastian told me today that he has to marry soon and produce an heir to carry on the family name."

He turned away from the screen to look at her. "He did, did he? Maybe you're on his short list."

Turning back, he continued, "Listen to this: *To answer your question, Inez was working as an archivist at a museum in Madrid when she died.*

"That means she would have had access to documents like the one in Reynaldos' room. Geoff must have told her the little he knew of the Sinclair family story in a weak moment, she stole the Spaniard's genealogy from Geoff's computer, then she went looking for Don

Alonso de Reynaldos in the museum's archives, where she stole the document."

A chill swept over her. "By going to Sebastian with your family story and the document, she signed her own death warrant. I wonder how much she asked for?"

"A lot, I'm thinking." He continued reading. "*Sebastian Reynaldos is the head of a major industrial conglomerate, which is about to enter into a merger with another group of companies headed by a very conservative CEO. This CEO has a daughter to whom Reynaldos is engaged to be married upon the completion of the merger.*"

She put her hands on Trev's shoulders as she read the lines. "What a jerk! Engaged to be married, playing slap and tickle with me, and having an affair with Megan, the tour guide."

"A bit of Jack the lad, as my dad used to say."

"I'll bet Sebastian walks the line in Spain, and he wouldn't want any bigamists falling out of the family tree at a time like this."

"There's more. *Will bring details with me. See you tomorrow. Geoff. P.S. An unexpected bonus. Will call your mobile number before I start south. Something big. BE CAREFUL WITH THIS GUY!*"

Trev printed out the information and backed up the message to a disk. They discussed the implications of Geoff's information and warning until it was time for Trev to leave.

She watched him shove a change of clothes into a small nylon bag. "I'll come with you part of the way to Avallen."

He zipped the bag and came to her. "Are you sure? You've been through a lot tonight."

She nodded and received an one-armed hug. "I think the exercise will help me sleep."

A short distance along the moor path to Avallen he stopped, told her she had come far enough in the dark, and put his arms around her. They stood on the path holding each other.

"Be aware, Ellie. I'll be back by noon tomorrow. We can't prove that Reynaldos fiddled with my brakes, or that he destroyed the documents in the church, and Inez's death is completely out of our hands," he said into her hair, "but we can bring this whole mess about the cross out into the open so the situation is defused."

"What about Geoff? If he suspects what Inez did or that Sebastian might have killed her..."

"If Geoff shows up before I get back, hand him over to Reilly and keep him out of sight. Maybe I can get him a desk job with the oil company in the Middle East, a change of scene. He'll get lots of rest and sunshine out there."

She leaned back and looked up at him. "Speaking of the Middle East, Trev. I've always wondered why you stopped writing to me when you were working there." The words, with their quiet urgency, hung in the darkness between them.

She heard his quick intake of breath, as if he was in sudden pain. His arms loosened around her. "It's all part of something else, Ellie, and I'd really rather tell you about it, and tell you many, many more things, when I get back."

Her body tensed and she let her arms drop away from him. "Your choice," she said simply, holding quick tears at bay.

Her imagination worked overtime at that moment. She guessed why he held back. It wasn't simply Sebastian's disturbances at Penwith. What if Trev was gathering his courage to tell her that, while he cared for her and was attracted to her, he had fallen in love while he was in the Middle East? Though the woman wasn't here with him now, he might still love her. She shivered. What if he had married this mystery woman?

Trev gripped her shoulders. "Not my choice, Ellie, the choice circumstances dictate. Be patient with me, love, please. We've both had things happen in our lives that we need to work through before we discuss them with each other. You've made a start, at least.

"With the house and Sebastian's unholy mess, I can't see straight for anger and worry. Add you, in the lovely flesh, into the mix and I can scarcely remember my own name. Right now, you're having a battle of wits with an unarmed man. We'll have lots to tell each other when things are calmer around here."

She pulled away from him. "Maybe we should just write it all down then exchange letters. We seem to communicate with each other much better that way." She turned on her heel and stalked away.

"Later, my love. I promise," he said to her retreating back.

She paused, turned, and gave him a reluctant okay before they each went their own way.

At the house, she said goodnight to Reilly then went into the library for more information gathering. Follow-up calls to the business owners she'd met with was on her list for tomorrow. Keeping her mind busy and off her new doubts and fears was the best medicine for the dull ache in her heart.

She glanced at the stack of books on local history on the library table. Then she remembered Trev telling her where to find one special book, written by an ancestor, which had a map of the secret passages in it. The book had a gold crest imprinted on its deep blue binding, and no title on its spine, he'd said.

She went to the dark corner where that book lived. A brass-shaded lamp there, fixed to built-in bookshelves with delicate fan-shaped carvings, cast a soft glow across the books' dark bindings. Her eyes and fingertips skimmed across the leather-bound spines marching away from her on both sides. She felt at home and in good company here, surrounded by Penwith's well-used books.

She made a little sound of satisfaction when she paused, then plucked the book from its place. She ruffled through the pages. It had been lovingly written and illustrated by a James R. Sinclair. As she touched its delicate paper, she realized the quantity of material available to her at Penwith about Penwith.

If Trev agreed, she could use these resources to research and write much more than simple brochures. A couple of book ideas immediately came to mind: a history of Penwith, which highlighted its connection with tin mining and fair-trading and included maps of the passages and a compilation of local families' stories about Armada survivors in their family trees. Her mind leaped ahead, one idea stepping on the heels of another. For another book, or booklet, she and Reilly could gather together recipes of dishes prepared in Penwith's kitchens through the centuries, like his pasties and damask cream. The books could be sold in the hall where the house tours would start out. Or, an interesting and practical line of items and souvenirs, created with a touch of class, might be sold in a little shop on the premises.

She and Trev and Reilly could organize the manufacture of, say...small sachets, assembled on a per-piece rate by local children and housewives and filled with potpourri made from herbs and flowers grown in the Penwith gardens. With careful planning, they might develop an exclusive line of Penwith herbal teas. By selling quality packaged teas and a selection of uniquely shaped sachets, including a cross if Trev approved, they could make the gardens pay for their upkeep and add to the profits.

She sat down at the library table, facing the door, and hurriedly jotted down her ideas to show Trev. How she would love to write the books and booklets and to manage the little shop she was imagining! If only she could stay at Penwith, if only she and Trev... But maybe Trev loved someone else.

"Your thoughts must be bittersweet, Ellie." Sebastian's voice came out of the shadows near the door.

Before she froze, her pen gouged into the surface of the paper and she yelped with fear.

Chapter Twelve

SEBASTIAN'S EYES GLITTERED in the shadows before he sauntered into the ring of light shed by the reading lamp on the oak library table. He stopped, standing very still, yet she sensed edgy excitement and satisfaction emanating from him. A sated look overlaid a hint of cruelty on his handsome features.

Her voice shook. "I thought you were...staying at The Fair Trader now."

"Only because your 'friend' asked me to leave. I did not like that. I came back for the rest of my things."

"How did you get in? Reilly checked all the doors."

"The little man? Not Sinclair?"

She didn't miss a beat. "Trev went up early. He has a headache."

"How very English of him."

"You didn't answer my question. How did you get in?"

"I still have the key I took earlier. I will leave it on the hall table. What are you writing?" He asked the question casually, but she heard the hard edge of interest behind the words.

"I'm jotting down ideas for promotional items to sell for the tours and the bed and breakfast. I want to suggest them to Trev when—tomorrow." She folded the sheet of paper, marveling at her newfound ability to speak while frightened witless.

Sebastian came around the table and held out one well-kept hand. "May I see your ideas?"

She shrugged and handed the paper to him.

He opened it, scanned its contents, and dropped it on the tabletop. "You are up late."

She glanced at the clock and couldn't believe what time it was. Trev's train had left hours ago. She put the paper inside the book with the maps in it and pushed back her chair.

"I didn't realize it was so late. I've packed a lot into the last few days, including going over a cliff." And a cathartic session with a reluctant kitten.

With one finger, he spun the book on the tabletop so he could read the title on the front. "Ah. This is the most comprehensive book on Penwith to be found in this place. It includes maps of the smugglers passages." His look and stance told her he would wait all night for her to speak.

She took her time. So, he'd thoroughly checked out the library at some point, which then made her wonder if he had checked out the passages. Here was an intelligent, ruthless man in a pretty package. He apparently didn't sleep, was head of a successful international business conglomerate, and yet, given the facts, she and Trev had somehow managed to underestimate him. Perhaps that was a grave mistake. She pushed back her chair again, seeking more room. He didn't give her any when she stood up.

Before she realized what was happening, he pulled her against him. "Ellie, Ellie," he whispered, his hands smoothing her spine. "Tell me you are not in love with Sinclair. Please." His hands moved to the curve of her hips.

Adopting her no-nonsense librarian's voice, she met his eyes squarely and opted for the truth. "Trev and I have never discussed anything between us except friendship. That's all. You, on the other hand, collect women the way you collect sixteenth-century Spanish jewelry. Since I refuse to be collected, please let me go."

He released her but he didn't step away. She did. "I'd like to go up now so I'll see you out."

He stopped her by wrapping the fingers of one hand around her upper arm, the thumb busy. "What are your plans for tomorrow? Perhaps we could meet for lunch."

With luck, he'd be busy answering questions at the local police station tomorrow at lunchtime.

She made up her plans as she went. "If it clears, I'll take a walk on the moor. There's a small lake nearby and a family of swans lives there. You can join me, if you like. We'll have a picnic."

His light touch on her arm turned into a punishing grip. "I suggest you stay away from the lake, Ellie." When she gaped at him, open-mouthed, he dredged up a smile that was more of a grimace. "You'll catch your death in Cornwall's changeable weather."

The pressure on her arm eased yet he didn't release her. She swallowed hard, and as she studied his unreadable eyes, a sudden, overwhelming sadness enveloped her. "Tell me what's wrong, Sebastian. Talk to me before you do anything stupid."

He smiled, without humor, but with an answering sadness evident in his features. "What is wrong, Ellie? Everything and nothing. I take advantage of opportunity, but my actions are seldom stupid. And since you know nothing about the Spaniard's cross, what could possibly be wrong between us? Sleep well." It sounded like a dare—or a threat.

He let go and she stepped away. "Do you have all your things?"

In answer he crossed the room and opened the library door, ushering her into the hall where his remaining bags sat near the front door. She was amazed that she hadn't heard his movements in the house.

"Since you are acting as chatelaine..." He handed her a key. "As you Americans say, I'll be seeing you, Ellie. Oh, before Sinclair sends you back to the United States, ask him to tell you about his trip to South America eighteen months ago."

"South America? You must be mistaken. Trev was on the other side of the world at that time in the...in the Middle East." Her voice died away on the last words.

"I think you will find he was not."

She didn't realize she was alone until she heard his car roar away. She forced herself to step up to the door. The key she held in her hand was Sebastian's room key, not a shiny new key for a modern lock on any of the venerable entry doors of Penwith. He could still get inside any time he chose. She locked the heavy front door, using both the new and old locks. Blinded by sudden tears and the sure knowledge that Trev had lied to her, she stumbled up the stairs.

She spent a restless night, missing Traveller's warm weight near her feet, knowing Trev wasn't in the house, fearing Sebastian was. She had shoved a chair under her doorknob but there was nothing she could do if Sebastian, who knew about the passages, used them to come to her room. She was sure her lame excuse about Trev not feeling well hadn't convinced him. Was he watching the house? Did he somehow know Trev wasn't there?

Reilly's rooms were in the cellars below the kitchen. His choice, Trev had told her. Reilly had said he would set his alarm to go off several times during the night so he could check the house and Traveller.

She slipped down the back stairs in the gray morning light. Reilly stood in the middle of the kitchen going over a shopping list. This touch of normalcy and his report on the kittens' health reassured her.

"Have you been to the shops already?"

"Oh, aye, twice. I forgot the half of what I wanted the first time." He moved to the refrigerator, taking out Traveller's cream and an egg basket full of brown eggs.

"No, thanks, Reilly. I'll have some of your Irish soda bread, and I can toast it myself. Is Trev back, or have you heard from him?"

Though it was unrealistic, she'd hoped to see him there in the kitchen, safely back from his mission in Treborne.

"Neither hide nor hair." The old man sighed then handed her the carton of cream and opened the pantry door for her. While he sorted out a colander full of potatoes, she filled the bowls Reilly had placed near Traveller's birthing area, one with cream, the other with fresh water. Another bowl, filled with dry cat food, stood within easy reach. A temporary litter box meant Traveller didn't have to leave her kittens.

Mother and babies appeared to be doing well. She stroked Traveller's head, told her again what a brave girl she was, and touched Chance's tiny black head with one finger. For Chance he was, in name and spirit, both for the dark-skinned truck driver who had kept her sane and for the kitten's tricky entrance into life.

They regrouped in the kitchen and she chattered, unable to stop herself. "Trev said he'd be back by noon or a little after. Maybe I'll walk to Avallen later and meet his train.

"Did you know that Sebastian came back late last night to get the rest of his things? He scared me silly. He gave me his room key when he left, but he still has a door key. You locked up before you went to bed, didn't you?"

Reilly had gone very white. "Aye, I did and I was up three times in the night to check all the doors and windows. I'll call the police if he shows his face here again. He's been put out of Penwith, hasn't he now?"

Occasional raindrops rattled on the kitchen windows. She balked at staying in the house all morning. Reilly didn't need her help with anything when she asked.

It was then she remembered the tale she had told Sebastian last night about her walk to the lake. The weather wasn't perfect for it. She was tired, and the atmosphere on the moor would be brooding on this day, yet she decided to go in spite of it all. She wouldn't think as much if she were in motion.

Rowing on the Penwith's lake was one of the things she had looked forward to doing. Sebastian's harsh words about staying away from there still rang in her ears. Why did her the mention of the lake last night evoke such an immediate and forceful response? Yes, a visit to the lake was called for, if for no reason except to defy Sebastian.

She ate her toast then went to her room for her rain slicker. Her hand froze in mid-reach when she found the blue and green slicker pushed to the side of the closet, out of sight. When it had dried after her trip to Penzance, she'd hung it in the middle of her large closet with her other things. So few of them needed to be hung up that she'd put all of them together so nothing would get pushed back and left behind when she packed.

It meant one thing. Someone, surely Sebastian, had been in her room recently. She hadn't locked her door since Sebastian left the house yesterday afternoon. If he'd felt confident enough to enter Penwith and snoop around her room last night while she was in the library, then he'd known Trev wasn't there. Maybe he'd searched Trev's room too. An awful fear for the cross began to gnaw at her.

She hurried down the hall to Trev's door. It wasn't locked, yet she definitely remembered Trev locking it when they left the room last night. She stood in the doorway, scanning the room for signs of disturbance. On heavy feet, she moved toward the fireplace. She went limp with relief when her fingers found the lumpy velvet pouch still in its hiding place under the mantel. Shaking, she returned to the kitchen.

She took a long look inside the closed key box, which hung on the inside of the pantry door. A lot of the hooks were empty. She didn't know if spare keys to the rooms had ever hung there. Reilly was watching her, a question in his eyes, so she plunged right in.

"Reilly, I think Sebastian searched my room, and probably Trev's, last night. I didn't know he was in the house until he came to the library. I saw Trev lock his door when he left last night, but it's unlocked now. Can you tell if any of the spare keys are missing from the key box?"

With trembling hands, Reilly checked the key box. "A couple are gone right enough, miss, your spare key and the guv's spare key—and one for the front door. Tha' Spaniard never came into my kitchen while I was here, I can tell you. Oh, but I'll be glad when the guv gets back."

Reilly looked smaller, whiter, and older this morning. She wanted to hug him but the thought of his reaction stopped her. Instead, she quietly noted his pale face and shaking hands.

"I'm taking a walk to the lake this morning. Would you like to come along? We'll feed bread to the swans and take our minds off this for a while."

In answer, Reilly pulled a cloth-covered bowl out of the oven. "I'm making Sally Lunn cakes, and I daren't leave them. You just come straight back here to me. You'll find some stale bread for the swans in a bag by the pantry door. The gulls were to have it anyway."

Ellie fetched the bread but hesitated to leave Reilly, Traveller, and Penwith. And Sebastian's parting shot still preyed on her mind. Maybe Trev hadn't answered her question about the Middle East last night because he really hadn't been there, as Sebastian hinted. But why did Trev lie to her about it at the time? If Trev were in love with someone else, did it matter whether the woman was Middle Eastern or South American? She couldn't let it go. She eyed Reilly, wondering if he knew about this mystery trip.

Her words tumbled out of her mouth. "Reilly, Sebastian told me to ask Trev about his trip South America just before my accident. I—"

A glass mixing bowl shattered on the flagstones, like the man who dropped it. Reilly's face turned from pasty white to gray as he leaned against the table. She helped him to one of the rocking chairs near the fireplace then knelt beside it, overcome with guilt that her words had done this.

"Should I call an ambulance? Or a doctor? Can you walk to the Land Rover?"

"I'll be fine, miss. Just give me a tick. Those sausages I had for breakfast aren't setting right with me. That's all."

She put aside the lie and made him a cup of tea. He was soon on his feet again, hard at work on his Sally Lunn cakes and insisting that she take her walk.

She finally left him, stepping out into the misty, blustery day. It looked like it might clear later, but she was no judge of Cornwall weather. She walked the same path she and Trev had traveled together the night before, until she came to the branch of track that turned away from the sea and wound its way across the green-and-tan moor to the lake.

The sharp tang of wind, still gusting from the sea, carried the cries of gulls inland. It teased her nostrils while her tongue sought one of the slightly salty drops of mist that clung to her cheeks. She remembered this place had frightened her the evening she'd arrived alone at Penwith.

The tea-colored lake water rippled in the wind. She recalled Trev's delight in describing to her this third notable Penwith exception to the geological rules. The lake formed eons ago where earth overlaid the small granite shield that also produced the moor-meadow.

The lake looked calm enough to row on. She freed the dinghy tied to a sturdy wooden dock and gingerly stepped into it. Its wood was darkened by the peat-stained water that collected in the lake before seeping down the valley and into the sea.

The physical act of rowing relaxed her and peace welled up within her. The oarlocks gave satisfying creaks with every stroke, marking time with her rhythm. While she rowed, she scanned the shores for the family of swans. Trev had promised her a picnic on the lakeshore and assured her that the swans expected a treat from everyone who visited them.

She made a little sound of delight when an armada of white and gray approached her bow. The parent birds sailed regally through the water with the darker cygnets paddling along behind. When one of the swans turned aside as they approached, Ellie saw two cygnets nestled comfortably on its back between its wings. Even these were tempted in for a swim when Ellie, who didn't ship the oars but let them rest in the water, tossed in the pieces of bread Reilly had saved. As she watched them scoop up the bounty, her thoughts turned to Trev and their unusual relationship.

She'd spoken the truth when she told him that life had gotten in the way of her coming to England—until she glimpsed death and lived. Before that, she had feared giving up everything she knew for something she couldn't understand. After the accident, she'd wanted Trev and no one else, when she lay half-conscious and hurting in the hospital for months. That trial by fire had given her the courage to take that step, meet Trev, touch him, and feel his touch.

As surely as she recognized her face in the mirror every morning, she sensed that everything she needed and wanted was here, in him. Her hope was that when this mess was cleared up he wouldn't hold back any longer. Her prayer was that he would finally share the feelings he hinted at with his kisses and his touch, and that he would unburden his secret, whatever it was. If he found love in her, not just physical attraction, maybe that love would be strong enough to overcome any lost loves he might cling to.

Stirring from her reverie, Ellie looked around the roughly circular lake. This was such a peaceful place. She saw no reason why Sebastian had ordered her to stay away—and it had been an order, probably a simple attempt to control her. From the moment they met, she hadn't shown him the respect his macho side expected and demanded of women.

Stinging rain riding stronger gusts of wind persuaded her to turn the dinghy back toward the dock. As she wrestled with an oar, she mentally waved a white flag to yet another day of Cornwall's unpredictable climate.

The oar on the right side wouldn't budge, upward or from side to side. When she lowered it then raised it again, it made contact with something. It must be catching a waterlogged piece of wood just below the surface, she guessed. Positioning the oar as vertically as she could, she tried to sweep it out from under the obstacle. That didn't work either.

She thought of taking the oar out of its oarlock to free it that way, but she hesitated. An amateur rower, she imagined dropping the oar into the lake and watching it float away while she bailed rainwater out of the dinghy. And bailing would be a wise course of action very shortly. Frustrated and worried, she leaned heavily on the oar, attempting to bring to the surface by brute force whatever was holding it down.

Instead, the dinghy careened sharply, and she slid sideways down the seat toward the water, watching its approach with dread. She feared a dunking; what she saw horrified her. The object that had weighted the oar so effectively broke the surface less than three feet from her face.

The body of a man bobbed face down in the dark water, a man with familiar, too-long blond hair, now peat-stained and speckled with tiny green leaves of a water plant.

She raised both hands to stifle her scream, yet Trev's name still echoed across the surface of Penwith's lake.

Chapter Thirteen

WITHOUT THE OAR'S support, the body slipped out of sight again beneath the surface.

Ellie's breath came in painful, gasping sobs. A sudden blast of wind and water spun the dinghy in a circle, completely disorienting her. She choked when rain drenched her face and poured into her mouth and eyes, temporarily blinding her. Where was he? She had to get him out of the water. Maybe she could help him... But in her heart she knew no life warmed that silent, cold shell. The only thing she could do was restore dignity to Trev. Reilly would know what to do.

The dinghy rocked crazily as her arms worked the oars independently of each other, slicing across the surface at odd angles. The swans squawked away toward safety, their outraged cries echoing her scream.

Her mind refused to take it in that Trev was dead. In fact, she suspected she would go crazy if she dwelled on it. Yet how could she not?

Hot tears mixed with cool rain on her cheeks as she rowed the boat with jerky strokes toward the shore. When she clambered out, her legs gave way. On her knees in the mud at the water's edge, she threw up on some nearby rocks.

When she could stand, she looked around her. In her panic and pain she had gone straight across the lake, away from the dock. She could see it, with the roof of Penwith showing behind it, in the distance. She set off around the lake's perimeter at a staggering trot.

Furze bushes, tinted gold with new yellow, pea like flowers, grew in three- to four-foot high, thick clumps on this side of the lake. They were interspersed with shaggy dead fronds of bracken and new spring fiddleheads. Wildly, she remembered Trev telling her about the popping sounds the ripe furze seedpods make as they burst on hot summer days. Now, the wiry evergreen shrubs' thorny branches simply tore at her clothes and ripped bloody gouges into her hands. She forced herself to look for softer areas of bracken.

Now she understood why Sebastian didn't want her to come to the lake, why he felt confident enough to enter the house last night.

Trev hadn't made it to the train. Sebastian had waited for him or met him by accident and murdered him in cold blood, dumping his body in the lake. And she had parted from Trev without hearing the words she yearned to hear.

She stumbled and fell when she remembered the edgy high emanating from Sebastian in the library last night. He'd probably just washed Trev's blood off his hands. If she'd known then...

A jolt of white-hot anger surged through her, and she realized that she, too, was capable of murder at that moment. Sebastian Reynaldos wouldn't get away with Trev's murder. And he'd never see the Spaniard's cross either, let alone touch it or possess it, even if she had to throw it off the cliff to prevent it.

The kitchen was dark and silent, making her tiptoe in, despite her sense of urgency. Her sodden, muddy shoes squished with each step, leaving a trail on the flagstones. Golden Sally Lunn cakes marched across a cloth on the sideboard. The potatoes were heaped in a colander in the sink. Reilly would never leave them that way, half of them in a pan of water and the others turning brown, unless...

Ellie's mind catalogued the possibilities as she glanced around the low-ceilinged room. In the half-light she could easily imagine she had stepped into another age, a darker age. Heavy silence sat upon the house like a hawk or some other bird of prey. The expectant quiet gave her chills.

A sound from the pantry rooted her to the spot. Whimpering. Her hand trembled as she reached out to open the now-closed door. Traveller meowed a greeting from her nest of clean cloths. The kittens suckled or slept in a line along her stomach. And Reilly sprawled in the corner, one hand wrapped around the long neck of a bottle of Irish whiskey.

She ran to him. "Oh, Reilly, no. Why?"

He opened his eyes. "Tha' bloody Spaniard," he sobbed. "'*Buenos dias*, little man. Have a drink with me,' he said to me. I recognized him, see."

His words confused her and made her more afraid. Would she ever learn the truth now about what Trev had been hiding from her?

He continued, his words slurred. "Geoff and the guv never saw him 'til the end. I did. At the Santa Maria oil field, from the cook tent. Just before the ambush. *El Halcon*. The Hawk."

The Spanish words tripped the memory that had eluded her earlier. Sebastian at the sale preview had said to her, '*You do not know who you are dealing with. I am not called El Halcon without reason.*'

"Where is he?"

"Don't know. Gone, I think. Don't know..."

"Hush now, Reilly," she said, easing the bottle out of his grasp. "You'll be all right again, I promise. Trev and I—" She gulped. "Annie and I will make it all right again. I'm going to lock us in then phone the police station in Avallen."

But the telephone that hung on the pantry wall was dead.

"I'm going to Avallen, Reilly. I'll bring help."

She locked the pantry door behind her then slipped the key into her jeans pocket. Her teeth chattered. The furze bushes had shredded her rain slicker, and the heavy rain had soaked her to the skin. She wouldn't take time to change into dry clothes now. But there was something she *would* do before she went to Avallen. For Trev. '*Go to Trev's room, get the cross, go to the police.*' The mantra played in an endless loop in her mind, giving her the courage to start up the dark back stairs.

She placed each foot with care on the wooden steps. From experience she knew the third one from the top gave the tiniest squeak. She stepped over it to the one above. The hall was still and thick with shadows. Instead of letting the door in the paneling thud softly behind her, she held onto it so it closed without a sound.

Her hand shook as she reached for the knob of Trev's door. What if Sebastian, searching for the cross, waited for her on the other side? She smiled grimly. If she was going to die by the same hand, then Trev's murderer would carry the marks of her death struggle for the rest of his life.

Taking a deep breath, she turned the knob. She sensed she was alone when she stepped inside. Silently she slid the ancient bolt home and turned the new lock as the tears came. Gulping them back, she lifted the handset of the telephone beside Trev's bed. It, too, was dead. Her picture sat beside it, angled toward the bed. She hadn't noticed it there before.

Her legs carried her in slow motion toward the fireplace. A flashlight sat on the mantel from the work in the passage, set aside today because of a death in a worker's family. Her frantic fingers found the hollowed out place under the mantel. Inside, still safe from Sebastian's hands, was the jumble of chain, precious stones, and carved gold that was the Spaniard's cross. Trembling, she put the chain over her head and tucked the cross beneath her shirt. Its weight and strange warmth between her bare breasts gave her small comfort now.

Sudden deep, racking sobs tore through her. To muffle the

sounds, she took a pillow off Trev's bed and buried her face in it. Catching his scent as she hugged it to her, she sank down into one of the chairs beside the fireplace.

She had shared more with Trev than she had ever shared with anyone. Yet there were just as many things about him, and about her, that they had been cheated out of discovering and sharing. Her hot tears mourned the love she would never know, except on paper.

In her misery, she didn't hear the scrape of stone on stone from the fireplace, didn't feel the cool moist air from the passage on her back, didn't realize she wasn't alone until strong hands closed over her shoulders and pulled her to her feet.

It was blue eyes she stared into over the top of the pillow, not brown. Its fluffy bulk, still jammed against her mouth, effectively muffled her scream. She watched in disbelief as familiar lips formed hot words.

"Ellie? What are you doing here? What's wrong?" A mixture of puzzlement, anger, and fear distorted Trev's handsome features. He clipped off his words, firing them from his mouth like bullets. "I'll kill Reynaldos if he's hurt you in any way."

She cast the pillow aside, and Trev's warm shoulder, firm with living muscle, replaced it in muffling her sobs, grateful prayers, and laughter. He staggered and they nearly bowled over into her chair's mate on the other side of the fireplace.

She couldn't get close enough to him. Everywhere his body fit against hers, she felt his life's blood pump beneath his skin, reassuring her he was alive.

Caught up in her adrenaline high, his lips sought hers, rough and tender at the same time. Like a thief, she stole warmth from his seeking mouth and reveled in her prize. When they broke apart, she caught a glimpse of his bewildered face before he pulled her to him again, smoothing her hair and whispering sweet words to her, until she regained control.

He eased her down into the chair behind her. His one tiny movement away from her made her cling to his hand with both of hers. She wouldn't let him go into the bathroom for a wet cloth or a glass of water for her.

"Tell me what's happened, Ellie. Slowly, but now, please." His gaze moved over her bloodied hands and tattered rain slicker. "Is the door locked?"

She managed one jerky nod of her head and, following his lead, spoke in a whisper. "I-I thought you were dead." Her teeth chattered and she stopped for a few seconds. "There's a b-body in the lake."

He slid off his perch on the arm of her chair to kneel on the floor in front of her. He stared up into her face. "A body? Are you sure?"

She looked past him to that awful moment at the lake. "H-He has white hair, j-just like yours." The tears started again.

"Geoff." Trev's voice broke on the word and fear mixed with sadness in his eyes. "Geoff is—was—a towhead like me. The boys at school teased us about looking like twins.

"We have to get out of here, Ellie. Geoff was supposed to take you and Reilly to safety last night. I just got back from Treborne. Penwith is closer than Avallen, so I decided to check the house. I'll get the cross."

She patted the front of her shirt. "I have it. I was taking it to the police, but I would've thrown it off the cliffs before I'd let Sebastian so much as see it."

"Well done." He kissed her scratched hands before pulling his own free. He rose and went to his closet. "We really didn't know who we were dealing with. Reynaldos is much more than just a descendant of the old Spaniard. The Spaniard's cross is mixed up with something else concerning me and Geoff and Reilly." He took out a heavy jacket then helped her peel off her rain slicker. The dry, warm jacket felt like a hug.

She reached into the corners of her mind and raked in her straying thoughts. "*El Halcon.* The Hawk." At Trev's gasp, she continued. "That's what Reilly called Sebastian just now. He said he recognized him from the Santa Maria oil field. Sebastian is—was—here, last night and today. He gave Reilly drink. He's sleeping it off in the pantry. I locked him in with Traveller and the kittens."

"The cruel, heartless bastard. I wonder if he used Reilly to find out Geoff was on his way so he could ambush him." He pulled her to her feet.

Her tears flowed anew as the words she said to Sebastian yesterday replayed in her head. "Maybe I did. I told him your old friend was coming today, but I didn't name him or where he was coming from. Sebastian went quiet and still when I said it."

"None of this is your fault, Ellie," he said as he comforted her again. "Let me tell you what happened. I've been a busy boy. Geoff called me on my mobile at the church in Treborne last night. He came via the Chunnel with someone he knew. He was in Avallen then and heading for Penwith. He told me what he didn't say in his e-mail about Reynaldos. I told him to get you and Reilly out of the house. He agreed, said his mobile's battery was low, and we were suddenly cut off. I tried to call the house but the phones were out of order. Reynaldos probably cut the lines. I borrowed the vicar's car, it broke down, so I started walking, hitching a ride when I could."

The light knock on Trev's door sounded like a cannon going off in the short silence that fell between them. Ellie's hand flew to her mouth to stifle the scream that hovered there. If she started screaming now, she would never stop.

"*Madre de Dios.*" Mother of God. Trev whispered the Spanish words then ran nimbly and silently across the room, picked up the chair at his desk, and slid it beneath the doorknob.

"Ellie? I know you are in there, *querida*," Sebastian's muffled voice came through the old wood. "You have left a trail of muddy footprints to this door."

Sebastian calling her 'darling' made her shiver. Trev motioned her toward the fireplace. She whimpered, realizing what he meant to do. He reached out to her but she backed away. He snagged her hand and pulled her toward him.

Outside Trev's door, Sebastian continued a one-sided conversation in silky tones that set her teeth chattering again. "The game is finished, Ellie. You know where the Spaniard's cross is hidden in Penwith. It belongs to me. If you help me find the cross, I will forgive your bad judgment in choosing Sinclair. I might even spare Sinclair when he shows up, if you cooperate."

Numb horror gripped her as Trev opened the fireplace panel. The blackness reached out for her and she moaned.

The sound of a key sliding into the lock drew Ellie's horrified stare away from the thick blackness of the passage to the door. She watched, mesmerized, as the knob turned slowly, first one way then the other.

What happened next was over in an instant, yet she heard and saw everything in freeze-frame action. A piece of the heavy wooden door between the old lock and the new splintered at the same moment an explosion sounded in the hall. A string of Spanish curses followed the shot. But the ancient bolt held and the desk chair held. More shots must follow, before he could reach a hand through to undo the bolt and move the chair, her dazed mind told her.

Trev took her by the shoulders and made her look at him. "I hope your fear of dying is greater than your fear of total darkness," he whispered. "Trust me, Ellie, and remember you're not alone. I'll be right beside you."

With that he shoved her ahead of him into the dark passage and closed the stone panel behind them.

Chapter Fourteen

IT WAS THE velvety blackness of her nightmares, so utterly black that she didn't know if her eyes were open or closed. The air she dragged into her lungs was thick with it and left her panting. She was dimly aware of Trev's arm supporting her as she fought for each breath.

He pulled her forward, down stone stairs, deeper into the darkness. The total absence of light and sound pressed against her eyes, her nose, her throat. The weight of her body was her only assurance that they hadn't plunged into black water.

Without warning, Trev's face leaped out of the darkness. He held up a long silver flashlight between them. It shone on their faces, lighting them like children trying to frighten each other with shadows.

"It won't take Reynaldos long to find the panel and follow us. I don't have anything to wedge against it on this side. We need the flashlight." He squeezed her. "Be brave, Ellie. The new lights aren't connected yet. It will slow him down if he follows in the dark."

Her mind snagged on the few words about the fireplace panel. "J-James Sinclair's book. Sebastian knows about the passage." She concentrated on Trev's face and on the curtain of light hanging in the darkness between them.

"And our boy's not stupid. You just disappeared from a locked room and left footprints leading into the fireplace. He'll have no problem finding the right spot to push on the panel."

She felt panic well up the moment she allowed her thoughts to stray to the suffocating blackness around them. She forced herself to respond to Trev and his words.

"There's a flashlight on the mantel. He'll use it." Her voice echoed eerily off the black stone walls.

"Damn!" Then Trev smiled and his white teeth sparkled in the light. "We'll be halfway to Avallen before he knows it. On the moor end of the passage near the sea is a locked door with bars on the outside. I have the key in my pocket. I left my bag there, with my mobile phone in it. We'll call for help. I hope Reilly is safe in the pantry for the moment.

"Now, we have to hurry. Concentrate on the light and squeeze my hand when you feel overwhelmed. And talk to me. Anything that comes into your head, just not too loudly."

He urged her forward at a lope, keeping a firm grip on her hand. The current of strength that flowed into her the first time they met flowed into her now like a storm tide. As the pool of light led them deeper into the darkness, she focused her attention on Trev's warm fingers wrapped around hers.

The passage ceiling was high enough for them to stand upright. She allowed one moment's thought for the vast weight of stone above their heads. The air was cool, damp, and surprisingly fresh. She breathed easier as the minutes passed. With that, the panic hovering in her chest settled to a manageable level.

Despite her movements, her teeth chattered and she shivered again. Trev's jacket had drawn dampness from her wet clothing. Her jeans, caked with mud, were cold and clammy against her thighs. Heavy with absorbed water, her nylon and suede running shoes felt like weights on her feet and still squished softly with each step. Her socks and underwear were full of grit. If she wasn't so afraid, she'd be miserable.

Her voice, surprising her, cut across this depressing line of thought. "You didn't have a chance to look at the records at St. Mary's in Treborne then?"

"Oh, but I did. When my train arrived last night, I discovered that St. Mary's roof had been damaged in a storm. It's being repaired in round-the-clock shifts. Due to the kindly vicar on duty, I was able to get in and do my research immediately. That's where I took Geoff's call.

"We were right. Elizabeth Sinclair and Don Alonso de Reynaldos were married on October 15, 1588, in the parish church at Avallen, verifying the old Spaniard's document. It was indeed her oldest brother who was the vicar at that time. He officiated, as you said, at the risk of his calling and his very soul. There were entries for the birth of Elizabeth Sinclair's son, Reginald, on August 31 and his baptism on September 15,1589, by the same vicar. I have copies of the entries in my pocket."

Her body warmed ever so slightly now with their exercise. Words poured from her. Her thoughts and voice turned to Sebastian, what he'd done, what he'd tried to do, the fire in his eyes when he spoke of the cross. She babbled but she didn't care. Her river of words and Trev's hand were the only things that held her in this world. If either stopped or were taken away, she was afraid she would go insane.

"With all the information we have, I still don't understand why

Sebastian would go to such lengths for the Spaniard's cross. Maybe his obsession with it has made him mentally unbalanced." Suddenly out of breath, she hoped Trev would now fill the darkness with his words.

He paused, dropped a quick kiss on her damp hair, wiped his forehead on the sleeve of his wool shirt, and moved on.

"Now that I know more about him, I'm sure he was mentally unbalanced long before he found out about the cross. When he and Reilly recognized each other, Reynaldos set about tying up loose ends, before the merger and his marriage take place. He came to England prepared to do whatever was necessary to get the cross then he realized he had some tidying away of his old life to take care of at Penwith as well. I underestimated him from the beginning because I didn't know who he was. The Spaniard's cross is only part of it."

Trev tightened his fingers around hers, and his voice filled with anger and pain. "I'm sorry you and Inez got dragged into this. You wouldn't be running for your life and she and Geoff might still be alive if I..."

Ellie returned the pressure of his fingers. Every word he said added to the puzzle. Why was he still reluctant to explain it all to her? "Don't blame yourself, Trev. I came unannounced. Geoff's path crossed Sebastian's in a moment when murder could be done. If Inez tried to blackmail Sebastian, then she brought about her own death."

"Reynaldos would have arranged to cross Geoff's path anyway, because he couldn't let him live. Just like he can't let me live, or Reilly," he whispered. "I'm still alive because he wants the cross, if he can get it. I suspect Reynaldos has a plan for Reilly and...me."

His unspoken, 'and you,' hung in the darkness between them. She tugged on Trev's hand and brought them to a halt, studying his face in the flashlight's glow. "Tell me about your loose ends from another life, Trev. You weren't in the Middle East, were you?"

"No. No I wasn't. I was someplace quite different."

"Tell me. Please, Trev, tell me now about South America, *El Halcon*, and the Santa Maria oil field, and anything else that needs to be said."

"We have to keep moving." He glanced behind them then urged her forward. "Believe me, I intended to tell you, but I wanted Reynaldos out of our lives first. I didn't know he was tangled in two threads of my life.

"Before your accident, I was with a crew, including Geoff and Reilly, that was being rotated off an oil platform in the North Sea. One of the men, an Australian nicknamed Roo, was a mercenary. He knew of a unit that needed a civilian oil crew, including a geologist, for a mission in South America. The three of us signed on as a lark. The money was good. Geoff and I needed the money, and we hoped it might keep Reilly sober.

"We were flown to the Santa Maria, a small oil field surrounded by jungle. The three of us, Roo, and the commander were the only British subjects in the unit. The mercs, lead by a second Australian named Clive, who was mad as a hatter, were there to secure and hold the field for the leader of the latest coup. We were an afterthought, under their umbrella of protection. Reilly became friends with the unit's cook. He spent a lot of time with him.

"The mission was orchestrated by a broker who arranged these things for rebel leaders. Everyone knew *of* him. He was a Spanish businessman, known in mercenary circles as *El Halcon*, The Hawk. He had a reputation for ruthlessness and for sending men to the highest bidder."

"Sebastian?" Disbelief echoed in her voice.

"Sebastian Reynaldos is *El Halcon*, the *arreglista*, the arranger, the man Geoff has been searching for in Spain. That's what he told me last night.

"Anyway, we were there a few months when another coup took place. Geoff, Reilly, and I were at the airstrip, picking up supplies. A helicopter sat on the runway near the supply plane. We started back, in an ancient Land Rover with a machine gun mounted on the back and a trailer attached.

"All hell broke loose. The oil field was under attack and we were driving right into it. We turned around to head back to the airstrip. Reilly manned the machine gun while I drove and Geoff fought to unhook the trailer. Just as he freed it, Geoff was hit. The pilot of the supply plane took pity on us and took us aboard.

"From our plane, I watched a truck pull up carrying three men wearing camouflage uniforms. Clive was driving. The man beside him was big, with hair and beard as black as the oil the Santa Maria field pumped. I'd never seen him before. Reilly said it was *El Halcon*. They boarded the helicopter and took off. The Australian abandoned his men and the civilians under his protection. Our pilot took off, too. We assumed the rest of the oil crew and the mercs were killed."

"Reilly said Sebastian was there, at Santa Maria, before it all went wrong. He said he recognized Sebastian, that Sebastian called him 'little man.' No wonder he acted so strangely after Sebastian came to Penwith."

"I wonder if that's what he started to tell me the night Traveller had her kittens?"

"If only we'd listened. Did you find out if anyone else survived?"

"No. When we got back to England, I visited the Home Office and gave a statement. After giving me a stern warning, which amounted to 'Don't do it again,' they told me there was nothing they could do. Foreign nationals, foreign country. They passed it on, anonymously, to someone at the United Nations, though. I told them that if they ever caught the broker or the Australian commander, I'd testify."

"So, when the Land Rover went over the cliff, I wasn't the only one to escape death for the second time in a little over a year. It's a shocking story, Trev, but why were you afraid it might change my opinion of you?"

She felt his shrug in the darkness. "Because I'm still alive and I didn't try to help the others. From everything I've written to you, would you ever have thought it was in me to join a mercenary unit?"

"As a *civilian*, Trev, doing your civilian job. And part of the reason you did it was for Reilly. You're not a trained soldier. If you'd made it back to the oil field, you'd be dead, too."

"That doesn't make it right."

"But it makes it *over*. Is that when you decided to renovate Penwith?"

"Yes. And as for why I didn't write... With a complete change of routine and by not writing to you for a while, I hoped that I might be able to see *us* more clearly. It worked. I came home to Penwith, took a leave of absence, put my bed-and-breakfast scheme in the works, and invited you over to help me with it. Then you had your accident. I was hip-deep in work and workmen and couldn't leave to come to you."

His teeth gleamed white in the darkness. "But here you are. And here I am. And I like that combination very much indeed. My invitation was a ruse to get you here, you know."

She grinned. "Was it? I'm glad."

The rock beneath their feet was wet now, and Ellie smelled the sea in the cool air of the passage. The icy puddles she stepped into sent fresh chills over her body. Trev's steady flow of words kept her calm and occupied her mind. She was grateful.

He pointed out brackets, refitted with flame-shaped bulbs, set into the glistening rock walls to hold torches so the smugglers could see to do their work. She'd welcome the yellow light of smugglers torches in the dark passage right now, or the fair-traders careful but purposeful steps on the stone floor.

She squeezed Trev's hand in gratitude when he continued. "The small coves and narrow inlets around Penwith were ideal for smuggling. When the wind, tide, and moon were right, the excise men were sent on a false trail or bribed. In 1856, the watch on the coasts passed to the Admiralty and fair-trading ended."

Ellie's wished-for smugglers' noises were swiftly all too real. A gunshot echoed down the passage in front of them. Water dripped somewhere close by in the following silence. They heard, faintly, a thud and a muffled curse in Spanish.

Trev mouthed to her, "Reynaldos. He's coming in from the moor end. He must have driven to it. But how the hell did he find the entrance?"

Panic welled up again. "I told you. James Sinclair's book. Can we go back?"

"I'll give odds that he jammed all the moving panels somehow so we can't get out the way we came in."

A few feet ahead was a boarded up area against the rock wall. Trev marched up to it and picked up a rusty crowbar that lay nearby.

"This goes into the Prudy's Hope tin mine," Trev whispered in her ear. "A backup escape route during the smuggling days. I sealed it off because of the shaft. If we break through into the tunnel, we can follow it to the ruins of the engine house in the cove and get out that way." Ellie held the light while Trev pried away boards firmly fixed into place across a wood frame anchored in the stone. The passage echoed with the screeches and splinterings of the wood as it reluctantly came away from the framework around the opening. So much for silence. Sebastian would know exactly where they had gone when he got to this place.

Trev opened a space just big enough for them to slip through. Sebastian would have to use his hands to make it wide enough to accommodate his large body. Trev threaded the crowbar through the belt loops on the back of his jeans. Ellie wondered if there were more barriers ahead or if he planned to use it as a weapon later on.

He held the light and steadied her as she put one leg through the opening then ducked under the boards above. She concentrated on the light and tried to find something to occupy her thoughts as she held the light for Trev to climb through.

What she thought about was the passage tours. She imagined a thick, clear acrylic sheet covering this opening into the mine. Soft lighting on the mine side, a figure or two denoting smugglers, some crates, and a few kegs stamped 'brandy' would set the scene. The tableau would add a new dimension to the tour of the passage. Another scene, behind the first and a little deeper into the tunnel, could be a tin-mining scene. She'd tell Trev later, if they got out alive.

The darkness had a different quality in the mine tunnel. The blackness was less dense. A muted roar floated up the narrow, steeply descending tunnel, and the smell of the sea was stronger.

She sensed Trev's urgency as he led the way, half-walking, half-sliding down the slippery descent. "In about a hundred feet, this section connects with the lift area where the miners descended into the shaft."

Ellie didn't hear sounds from behind them, but with every step the muffled roar grew louder. "What's that noise?" she finally asked.

She slid and Trev gripped her arm. "The workings extend below the sea floor. That's the ocean pounding the cliffs."

Ellie gasped and stopped short. Trev gently pulled her forward.

What working conditions had the Prudy's Hope tin mine offered the Cornish tin miners? They worked for a pittance, always aware of the sea just above their heads. The constant roar of waves breaking against the cliffs wouldn't have let them forget and neither would the saltwater seeping into nooks and crannies all around them. Yet this rock had been their only protection from the sea, just as it now was theirs.

They rounded a sharp turn and came out into a cavern. Trev flashed the light around it. To the left stood the rusty metal framework of the old cage lift, installed by a progressive Sinclair owner to replace wooden ladders, which had taken the miners even deeper into the earth's bowels, beneath the sea. A wood plank floor covered the shaft opening.

"It looks solid enough," Trev said, "but it's rotten right through. It won't take any weight at all. We'll have to walk around the edge of the planks where they rest on a lip of rock around the shaft."

On the other side of the cavern, across the plank floor, was another boarded up area—with daylight seeping through the cracks between the boards. For one desperate moment Ellie wanted to run toward the light, but the steady pressure of Trev's hand on hers made her think clearly again.

"Keep your back and your heels against the rock wall, but don't hold yourself so rigidly that you lose your balance. I'll lead the way."

Trev adjusted the crowbar in his belt loops then cautiously stepped onto a rotting plank. Ellie took a deep breath and followed. A hollow plunk sounded as a piece of wood underneath broke away and slithered down the rock ledge of the shaft lip. She pulled back, perspiration breaking out along her upper lip.

"It's all right," Trev reassured her. "I helped my father build this cover when I was ten. There's a good eighteen inches of solid rock the whole way around most of the edge."

"*Most* of the edge?" There was a definite squeak in her voice.

She stepped onto the plank again and inched sideways, to the right, following Trev, as they started around the perimeter. He tested each plank with his foot before giving it his full weight. Ellie then stepped onto the plank he had just left. Frightening little creaks and groans from beneath their feet marked their progress. Like wind-up toys, they sidestepped their way to a bulge in the rock halfway across.

Trev leaned forward to look around the mass. "Stay here until I go around it."

"No," Ellie said and pulled on his hand. "We go back or we go forward, but we do it together."

Trev looked into her eyes then raised the hand he held to his lips. "Together, then."

Trev's lips on her skin contrasted with Sebastian's touch the way a sunlit day on the moor would measure up to this tunnel. Warm and sweet and full of promise, they shot a delightful sensation up her arm then through her, all the way from her damp, wild hair to her wet feet. She shivered, but not with cold. At that breathless moment Trev could have led her anywhere. She prayed he would have that chance to lead in the future, and she to follow.

Her legs trembled as she followed Trev out onto the shaft cover. One thick, black plank was split, and he gingerly stepped over it. They were more than eighteen inches out on the planks at the farthest point of the bulge. The wood actually looked more solid here as they stepped around the outcropping of rock. They maneuvered around one more split plank before they inched back toward the rock wall. Then, their feet were once again on planks resting on solid rock.

The shaft cover curved around toward the boarded up opening at the front of the cavern. When they stepped off rotted wood onto solid stone, Ellie rested in Trev's arms for a moment, her head against his chest.

Now. She had to say the words now. They nipped at each other's heels in their haste to be said, propelled by her sense of urgency. "We have to tell each other the things that need to be said, Trev. I came to England to see if I love you as much in person as on paper. I do." Only then did she look up into his eyes. The relief and joy she saw there reassured her that she was loved in return.

He placed a quick, searing kiss on her lips. "I planned candlelight and soft music to tell you this, Ellie. I invited you here for the same reason. And I love you, too." He let go of her and slid the crowbar out of his belt loops, tearing at the boards covering the entrance into the engine house in the cove.

Soon, a stiff breeze off the sea swirled around them, and sunlight poured through the gap, lighting the whole cavern. The opening was big enough for them to crawl through, when Sebastian's voice froze them in place.

"How very efficient, Sinclair. I can, as Ellie taught me to say, 'Kill two birds with one stone.' But first you will give me the Spaniard's cross."

Chapter Fifteen

TREY'S EYES MET hers for a split second before his shifted pointedly to the ragged opening. He gave a tiny jerk of his head toward the expanse of daylight.

She realized what he planned. He would draw Sebastian's attention and his gunfire, giving her time to escape into the engine house. Well, he'd have to think of something else. She thought she'd lost him once, and she never wanted to feel that way again.

As they slowly turned toward Sebastian, Ellie locked her arm with his. "Together," she told him in a whisper. He smiled down at her crookedly and gave a resigned nod of his head.

The acoustics of the rock cavern were so good that Trev didn't raise his voice. "You think I have the Spaniard's cross with me? There are a thousand hiding places in Penwith. I've hidden it so you'll never find it." His voice held a tentative note that Sebastian wouldn't miss.

"I will risk losing the cross to be rid of you, Sinclair, and all you stand for. But since I sense its presence against warm, soft, satiny skin, I would say Ellie is wearing it." He smiled when Ellie gave a start. "Don't play foolish games with me, Sinclair."

Sebastian's voice was tense, excited. Ellie realized he was capable of pulling the trigger any second.

"Does *your* side of the family have a story about the cross, Reynaldos? Come over and we'll compare them, shall we?"

She understood what Trev was trying to do. If Sebastian thought they'd crossed the shaft cover....

Sebastian sneered. "Much like yours. An ancestor of mine gave it to an ancestress of yours, for services rendered." His lip curled on the last three words, belittling that long-ago gesture of love, twisting the reason behind it. "Now I will reclaim the cross and take it back to Spain, where it belongs."

Trev's hand convulsed around her fingers in his struggle to let the words pass unchallenged. The tiny hairs on the back of Ellie's neck stood on end. In the light from the opening, even across the width of the shaft cover, she saw the unnatural gleam in Sebastian's eyes. *Tyger, Tyger, burning bright*. Sebastian was totally out of control, or he was totally mad.

When Trev spoke, she knew he had lost the battle to stifle his emotions. "We're talking about Don Alonso de Reynaldos and his *wife*, Elizabeth Sinclair Reynaldos, are we not?" he prodded, insolence in his tone.

Sebastian bared his teeth in the semblance of a smile, a smile that didn't alter the look in his eyes. "Ah, you know about that travesty of a marriage, do you? It is, of course, invalid since they were not married by a priest."

Trev shrugged and his voice hardened. "I also know about the document in your room, written by the old Spaniard, which you're so desperate to suppress. The good Don took the coward's way out, despite all his fancy language about the cross. He was already married, yet he took another bride when he returned to Spain."

Sebastian grew in size as he puffed himself up with pride. "Don Alonso de Reynaldos was an honorable man with a misplaced sense of duty. He owed Elizabeth Sinclair nothing; their *marriage* was a mere liaison. His legal bride was chosen by his family. The document was a..." He hesitated, searching for the right word to dismiss that long-ago love. "...a sentimentality."

Trev's bark of laughter echoed in the cavern. "Sentimentality? The document, the marriage record, and the birth and baptism records of their son will stand up in court in any country. I wouldn't have tested them, Reynaldos, but now you've made me angry."

"You come to anger too late. They are gone, or soon will be. You will never have the chance to test them, Sinclair." Sebastian's fingers shifted on the gun.

The movement made Ellie find her voice. "Your little act of vandalism in the church was in vain, Sebastian. Preservation copies of the parish records are stored in Treborne. We have copies of those and photocopies of the document you had in your room. It's a stalemate. Please, can't we sit down together and talk about this? Let's all go back to the house."

Ellie held her breath when Sebastian trained the gun on her. Whatever immunity she'd had because of his attraction to her was at an end—and still he didn't step onto the shaft cover.

"The records you carry with you now will be destroyed here. And I will burn Penwith to the ground before I leave, just to be sure. How dare you search my room?"

"How dare you search mine?" she shot back.

Her thoughts turned to Reilly and Traveller and the kittens, their little family, hers and Trev's, locked in the pantry. She prayed that if the opportunity arose, she'd find the courage to do whatever was necessary to get everyone out of this alive. Then hot anger at this man and his obsession and his dirty secrets suddenly burned within her. The tiny spark grew beneath the Spaniard's cross.

"There will be no compromise, Ellie, and how can it be a stalemate when I hold the gun? I will destroy the records in Treborne, now that you've told me about them. All records and references to the cross will be obliterated. I confess a desire to possess the cross for my own pleasure. I can forego that pleasure, however.

"You chose the wrong partner in this game, Ellie. What a waste. I could have taught you many things, like how to please me. And I would have enjoyed showing you Spain."

Every muscle in Trev's body tensed at Sebastian's words. "What makes this whole affair so stupid and unnecessary is that if I had stumbled onto the records on my own, or if I had been told about them, it would be just another chapter of a very private family story. Why have you came looking for the cross now, *cousin?*" He spoke sharply and the gun's black hole once again pointed at him.

Ellie sucked in a breath. She understood Sebastian's warped sense of pride. Softly she repeated his words back to him. "Pride," she said, heaping amazed disbelief onto the word. "Pride is everything to a Spaniard."

Sebastian silently studied Trev, like a predator ready to swoop upon its prey, not to kill out of necessity but for the pure satisfaction in the bloodletting. His face had changed subtly when Trev called him cousin. It was harder and more determined.

"*Touché*, Ellie. I have admitted I am curious about this cross, rumored in my family to be of great beauty and superb craftsmanship. But of more importance, I cannot risk being an object of idle curiosity or ridicule in my country, especially now. If the documents came to light, if it became known that I do not possess the cross, should a court decide that you are the legal descendant..."

"The merger? You're justifying what you're doing, what you've already done, because of a business merger?" Her words burst forth without thought about the consequences. "You've committed two murders and attempted another because a family scandal might mess up a business deal and tick off the conservative fiancé who's part of the package?"

Sebastian ignored her now. "You *have* been busy, Sinclair. Do you realize what you've done by telling Ellie everything? Now I must create a murder and a suicide for a pair of star-crossed lovers, one of whom is mentally unbalanced as the result of a car crash."

Trev's body quivered as he unleashed his anger. "I've had to tell Ellie very little. She was right by my side when I discovered most of it. That includes being in the Land Rover when it went over the cliff.

"So, damn and blast you and your merger, Reynaldos! Where was your sick sense of pride when you murdered Geoff and threw him in the lake like he was a sack of garbage? Where was it when you fiddled with my brakes, and when you killed Inez Concepcion the same way?"

Sebastian's face paled and he tightened his grip on the gun. "Inez Concepcion was a blackmailing little tart. What she knew, the boyfriend must surely know."

"What about the men at the Santa Maria oil field? What's your excuse for letting them die?" Ellie heard herself say.

Sebastian concentrated his hate on Trev. "That, too, Sinclair? I needed no excuse. They were expendable. I recognized the little cook when I first came to your house. His reaction to me told me I was correct. Clive had told me about the three of you who stuck together at Santa Maria. I had Geoff's name from Inez and I certainly knew yours. When I checked my records in Spain via computer, from your own library, there you both were. And the little man. You were all condemned from that moment. And from something I overheard, I knew you would all soon be together again. Here."

Ellie watched Sebastian's tension and excitement build. He would pull the trigger without crossing the shaft cover. If he concentrated on her, maybe they had a chance, a slim one. First she had to get Trev out of the light that silhouetted them. A small rusty piece of machinery stood off to Trev's right. Maybe....

Trev spoke before she could act. "So we're nothing but loose ends from your dirty little sideline? If you want the Spaniard's cross, then come over here, *cousin*. Will your pride allow you to look into my eyes when you murder me?"

Her warning was a tiny smile that lifted the corners of Sebastian's full lips.

Using her right hip and both hands, Ellie shoved Trev aside just as Sebastian fired. Trev slammed into the rock wall beside them while echoes of the gunshot reverberated in the cavern. Ellie screamed and involuntarily covered her head, not knowing if each blast was a new bullet meant for her or merely an echo.

When the noise stopped, she half turned with a sob and reached out a hand toward Trev. He held his left shoulder, while pain, regret, and sadness showed in his eyes. But her aim had been true. He was partially hidden from Sebastian's aim by the little piece of antique equipment.

She turned her gaze on the man still standing. "Sebastian, you wretched man, look what you've done."

Then she saw him through a red haze of flaming anger. The words of her prayer came back to her: whatever she had to do to save them. She would play her part well, so they could live. Sebastian hesitated, watching her closely as she felt a change come over her. She imagined Traveller in temptress mode.

"You win, Sebastian." She said the hated name on a purring note. "And to the victor go the spoils. The Spaniard's cross. And me," she continued in a breathless voice.

She eased up onto the edge of the shaft cover and slowly unbuttoned her flannel shirt. Sebastian's lips parted slightly, his tongue darting out to wet them.

She grasped the edges of the shirt with both hands and shrugged it off, and Trev's jacket along with it. The Spaniard's cross rested in all its glory just below the firm, generous mounds of her bare breasts, pointed with the chill of the cavern.

Sebastian gasped. Trev gasped. And the gun lowered. The flashlight from Trev's mantel wavered in Sebastian's hand as he focused its failing beam on the golden beauty of the Spaniard's cross, revealed to him for the first time. She looked down. The cross and its chain glittered and gleamed below and between her breasts as if they were in a spotlight.

"*Madre de Dios*," Sebastian whispered raggedly.

"Come on, Spaniard," she said in a voice hoarse with fear. "Come and collect the spoils of war."

Mesmerized by the treasures she had revealed to him, Sebastian stepped up onto the rotten shaft cover. She knew if he could think at all, he thought they had crossed the cover ahead of him.

Don't look at his feet! She shivered with the knowledge that she was tempting a man to his death. *Please, Sebastian, drop the gun and I'll tell you to stop and go back*, she begged him silently. He hesitated when the cover creaked. Trembling, she raised her arms to him in invitation and he moved toward her again.

"This is meant to be," he whispered. "You and the cross are meant to be mine, Ellie. Something in you calls to me from across a great expanse of time. Against my will, I want you," he ended hoarsely.

She held her breath, rigid with fear and anticipation, as Sebastian advanced, without hesitation now, across the creaking planks. His eyes were fixed on her face now rather than the Spaniard's cross. As tears spilled down her cheeks, she prepared herself for what must happen if she and Trev were to live.

He was halfway across when the planks gave way beneath his feet, a hangman's trapdoor. At the crucial moment Ellie threw herself back and to her right, out of the light, behind the scant protection of the ancient machine, and onto Trev's legs.

In the seconds before Sebastian silently disappeared beneath what was left of the shaft cover, he shot wildly in their direction, determined that they should die even as he was falling to his own death in the Prudy's Hope shaft.

She shoved herself up along Trev's body, full length, shielding him from the ricochets of the bullets zinging around the cavern. To protect their hearing, she pressed the left side of her head against Trev's left ear then covered their exposed ears with her hands.

"*No tengo mas que darte*. I have no more to give thee." She said the words over and over and over to mask the sound of the last plank crashing in after Sebastian.

In the deafening silence that followed, she sat up on Trev's lap. His eyes held hers. Then his voice, hoarse with pain and breathless with something else, said, "I couldn't wait to see what you would do if he made it across."

Chapter Sixteen

ELLIE, CURLED ON the sofa in Penwith's sitting room, learned two things after drinking several cups of strong, sweet tea generously laced with brandy. One, the bullet had passed through the fleshy part of Trev's shoulder. And two, her bones really hadn't dissolved. They had taken up their duties again.

The hollow, shocked feeling lessened in the warmth and security of Trev's nearness. She could think about what happened in the mine without crying or trembling now.

The police had questioned them, together and separately, after Trev told them about Geoff's body in the lake, and about Sebastian's body at the bottom of the Prudy's Hope tin mine, and about Inez Concepcion's accident in Spain.

Annie, who had returned early to Avallen as sirens and flashing lights headed for Penwith, made gallons of tea then went downstairs to comfort Reilly. Traveller rested with her kittens in the pantry. At last she and Trev were alone.

She pulled a blanket closer around her and leaned deeper into the curve of Trev's right arm. A brisk fire in the fireplace took the chill off the damp evening.

Trev made short work of her remorse at having lured Sebastian to his death. "He would have crossed the shaft cover anyway, Ellie. You just figured out a way to make him do it without shooting you first. He *had* to cross it in order to finish me off, take the cross, and make it look like one of us had committed suicide. He couldn't do any of that from where he was. Now stop and think about what I've just said. You saved our lives, love."

She looked up at him. "You mean like you and Geoff and Reilly saved each other at the Santa Maria oil field?"

She watched shock zing through him. When it reached his eyes, he said, "I suppose we did save each other. I never thought of it that way before."

Trev had refused to go to the hospital, take a pain pill, or leave her and Reilly and Traveller for even a short period of time. She had transferred the cross to his neck after the ambulance attendants patched him up then left, and after Trev's GP arrived, undid what the ambulance men had done, redid it, shot him full of antibiotics, and left. The cross now rested inches from her eyes.

"Will you claim the Reynaldos' 'lands and fortune,' now that you're the only living Reynaldos descendant?" she asked.

"Never. I don't want anything associated with Reynaldos to touch Penwith ever again. With hard work, we'll manage quite nicely without his blood money."

"We," she repeated softly, savoring the word.

"Yes, we. And it's time to tell you the rest of the story about the Spaniard's cross." Trev shifted uncomfortably and cleared his throat.

"Will you please take a pain pill? I can see you're hurting."

"Please, be a good girl and listen to this. I've been panting to tell you and now that the time is right, you want to knock me out with a pain pill."

"Sorry, my love. I'll listen. Then you'll take a pain pill?"

He laughed and squeezed her. "Agreed.

"The Spaniard's cross is an important part of a wedding tradition in my family," he began. "As the first-born son, and only child as it turned out, I was handed down the cross by my father to give to my bride."

She opened her mouth to speak, so he hurried on. "The family legend says that if a Sinclair bride wears it on her wedding day and wedding night, there will be sons to carry on the Sinclair name."

Trev's tanned cheeks darkened with embarrassment and he squirmed, but not from pain. She watched in amazement.

He swallowed and his voice dropped to a whisper when his eyes met hers. "It's magic has worked for over four hundred years, Ellie. There have always been Sinclair sons." He let go of her and, one-handed, he took the Spaniard's cross from around his neck and slipped it over her head. "Will you wear it on our wedding day and wedding night, Ellie?"

Her heart did acrobatics beneath the warm weight of the cross. "Are you asking me to marry you, Trev?"

"Yes, I am. I know it's crazy to fall in love through letters, but we did. So...please?" The last word was spoken by an unsure little boy.

She couldn't resist. "Despite the fact that Sinclair sons usually marry blondes?"

He was confidant again, and the look in his eyes made her knees turn to Reilly's damask cream. "You could be bald for all I care. Did you ever doubt, since we exchanged those first letters, that there was something special between us? I have loved you forever, Eleanor

Elizabeth Jaymes Sinclair."

She lifted the cross away from her shirt and positioned it in the palm of her left hand so that its gold touched the gold of the birthstone ring Trev had given her. At that moment, she felt kinship with Elizabeth Sinclair, the girl who had lived and loved so long ago. Because she, Ellie Jaymes, in this century, in this time, was giving her love to a stranger she understood with her heart.

"And I have loved you forever, Trevor Reginald Sinclair," she whispered to Trev—and to the imagined shadows of the young lovers watching them from the flames in the fireplace. "Yes, I will marry you, Trev. Bad rice, bad rice," she threw in for good measure, before she let the cross slide out of her hand.

She wasn't at all surprised when, in the next instant, she glimpsed the cross capture the firelight and burn between them with a flame of its own. And just before Trev made the world fade away, she heard faint echoes of murmuring laughter, and with them the sounds of the sea.

~ * ~

Cornish Recipes For Damask Cream And Pasties

These Cornish recipes use cream and butter. I've adapted them to more healthful ingredients. If you want the full impact on your taste buds and your arteries, use cream and butter. I've never tried Sally Lunn cakes. Too complicated. Reilly has more patience—and a better hand with dough.

DAMASK CREAM (Junket)
2 c. milk (or light cream)
3 T. fine sugar, heaped (2 if using cream)
1 t. vanilla (or 2 t. rosewater)
Junket® Rennet Tablet,
crushed & dissolved in 1 T. cold water
Nutmeg or mace for garnish

Optional:
4 T. cream
1 T. fine sugar
1 t. vanilla (or rosewater)
Red rose petals

Dissolve the sugar in the milk and add the vanilla. Bring the milk mixture to lukewarm (110 degrees) temperature. Stir in the tablet dissolved in water. Pour into a serving dish or single-serving dishes. Sprinkle with nutmeg or mace. Serves four.

Optional: Before serving mix 4 T. cream with 1 T. fine sugar and vanilla and pour over top. Garnish with red rose petals.
In Cornwall this is served with a layer of clotted cream on top.

CORNISH PASTIES
Any meat and vegetable combination or fruit combination can be used in this pasty crust. It's said the devil never ventured into Cornwall in case the Cornish decided to try a 'devilly' pasty!

PASTRY

4 c. flour
2 c. butter-flavored vegetable shortening, butter, or margarine
1/2 c. ice water
pinch of salt
(Or, buy four flat, ready-made pie crusts!)

Mix the salt into the flour and add the shortening. Work the shortening into the flour completely with fork or hands. Add the ice water until a smooth dough forms.

FILLING
Mix together:
1 lb. raw lean chopped beef (hamburger)
2 med. finely chopped raw potatoes
1 med. finely chopped raw onion
1 T. chopped fresh herbs (parsley, chives, basil)
salt and pepper

Roll out the pastry to 1/4-inch thick on a floured surface. Cut into four dessert-plate sized circles. On each circle put a layer of the meat mixture, off center. Moisten the edges and fold over. Press then crimp the edges with a fork or your fingers. Make a small slit on top—and add an initial on one edge, if you like. Place on a baking sheet and start out in a 400 degree oven until the pastry is pale gold, then lower heat to 350 degrees for about 40 minutes. At the point where the oven temperature is lowered, you can brush the tops with a beaten egg for a glaze, if you like.

Makes 4. I serve these with gravy on the side, as they can be a bit dry.

Sharon K. Garner

Sharon K. Garner enjoys writing stories about love and danger set in exotic locations. A former library cataloguer and newspaper proofreader, she keeps her hand in with freelance proofreading/light copyediting.

She lives with her welder/EMT husband of many years, a man who no longer flinches when asked such questions as "How long does it take to bleed to death?" and "How can I disable a big piece of equipment?" Two demanding cats with opposite personalities complete the household.

In her free time, the author reads English mysteries and regularly prances around the living room doing walk aerobics, all the while keeping an appreciative eye on her small collection of Tiffany-style lamps and her significantly larger collection of crystal figurines.

Visit hr at: http//www.sharonkgarner.com